RIDING FENCE

•

A.H. Holt

AVALON BOOKS
NEW YORK

© Copyright 2006 by A.H. Holt
All rights reserved.
All the characters in this book are fictitious,
and any resemblance to actual persons,
living or dead, is purely coincidental.
Published by Thomas Bouregy & Co., Inc.
160 Madison Avenue, New York, NY 10016

Library of Congress Cataloging-in-Publication Data

Holt, A. H. (Anne Haw)
    Riding fence / A.H. Holt
        p. cm.
        ISBN 0-8034-9801-2 (acid-free paper)
    I. Title.

    PS3608.O494358R53 2006
    813'.6—dc22
                                    2006009967

PRINTED IN THE UNITED STATES OF AMERICA
ON ACID-FREE PAPER
BY HADDON CRAFTSMEN, BLOOMSBURG, PENNSYLVANIA

For my brother Richardson (Rick) W. Haw, IV,
who lives in beautiful East Kansas.

Chapter One

Dan Smithson lay back on the blankets to prop his head on his saddle, glad to stretch out. He twisted and turned, trying to get comfortable. Suddenly he lunged to his feet, lifted his blanket and ground sheet, and brushed several rocks and twigs from the ground. When he finished brushing the area clean, he turned to check that his pony was still in sight and lay back down.

The dying fire painted his tanned cheekbones a deep red. His eyes were as black as his hair. Thoroughly tired and sleepy, he pulled one of the blankets around his shoulders and watched the moon come up through the canopy of leaves as he waited for sleep.

The sound of his horse munching on the tall grass down by the creek was comforting. He closed his eyes and listened to the night sounds. The water in the little creek made a soft murmuring as it flowed over rocks.

After a few minutes Dan realized he heard something else

as well—some sound that didn't to belong in the woods. At first he dismissed it as a tree branch or leaves moving in the wind, but when he opened his eyes and glanced up, the leaves on the tree above his head were still. No wind stirred.

Turning his head from side to side, he sat up and held his breath to listen. He heard the strange noise again—it was a soft whining and a sigh.

It almost sounds like someone crying.

He had started out from the Triangle Eight ranch house a little after dawn that morning. His regular job required him to inspect the boundary fence from the northwest corner of the property all the way to the south line shack, then back to the ranch house along the center line fence. He watched for weak or broken places in the wire or leaning posts that cattle sometimes pushed over. He expected to spend this night in the line shack and then ride as far as Ma Hainey's place before suppertime the following day.

Like most riders, he always carried a few supplies for emergencies, times when he had to camp out, but he hadn't counted on having to use them on this trip. There were always plenty of rations stored in the line shack in case any rider had to stay out overnight and needed them. Dan counted on reaching the shack where he would have a stove to cook his supper on. At the cabin he would have a coffeepot with plenty of coffee and all the firewood he needed, already cut and dry. More than that, he had counted on being in time for supper at Ma Hainey's place the following night. In his estimation, that woman's cooking beat any other he'd ever eaten.

The sections of fence he passed by the first half of the day looked fine and he thought he would have little trouble keeping to his schedule. A little after noon—to his consternation—he found posts pulled out of the ground and a long section of the wire knocked flat. When he dismounted and examined the fence closely he could see that none of the wire in the downed section was broken or cut.

Strangely, someone had taken the time to work eight fence posts loose from the dirt, pull them up out of their holes and lay them down on the ground. That pulled the wire down flat at the same time. It didn't make sense to Dan. Cowhands always carried a pair of wire cutters. Rustlers especially always carried wire cutters. They were one of the basic tools of their business.

It cost Dan several hours of backbreaking work to repair the fence so it would hold cattle if they took it in their heads to push against it. He knew he didn't have to worry about horses trying to get through the wire. They were smart enough to know the stuff would cut them up if they pushed against it, so they left it alone. It was getting near sundown when he finished resetting the posts and tightening the wire enough so no stock could wander through.

Even though it was late when he finished fixing the fence, Dan naturally set out to discover why it got pulled down like that and who was responsible for doing such a thing. The tracks on either side of the opening made it plain that a big bunch of cattle and as many as a dozen horses had passed through the gap in the fence, and they couldn't have done it without human help. The tracks were still fresh. He was sure they had been driven through the gap only a few hours before he got there.

The rustled stock left a trail heading west, over toward Elk River. After examining the tracks closely, Dan decided that the animals were being driven by at least three men. All of them rode newly shod horses.

He studied the situation a few minutes and decided he had best follow the trail of the cattle and horses instead of continuing on to complete his routine check on the fence. The rustlers hadn't been gone but a few hours, and even if they were pushing the herd along at its best pace, he knew he would likely catch up with them in no more than a day.

At first, the tracks led him on a direct route west. Later, they turned north on a path to intersect the main road to Wichita. He felt sure he would lose the tracks when they reached the road. It made sense that the men driving the stock would turn onto the main road going one way or the other. He expected to see their tracks mingle in with everybody else's and virtually disappear, but to his amazement they didn't turn either east or west, but continued on in the same direction—straight across the road and on toward the north.

Dan pushed his horse to a long trot and rode until almost dark. Finally he turned off the trail into a little clump of sycamore trees and elderberry bushes.

Me and this horse have worked enough for one day.

He had left the Triangle Eight's corral that morning before sun up, and he felt whipped. He knew he couldn't take a chance on overworking his only horse when he was this far away from home, either. The men driving the herd would have to stop and rest. He figured they had probably already stopped for the night. Horses and cattle needed rest as well as men. He planned to grab a meal and a few hours sleep then get right back on the trail at dawn.

Ducking his head to the side to avoid a low limb, he guided his horse into the coolness of a grove of oaks. His chest and shoulders still felt warm from the late evening sun, but deep shadow already covered most of the ground under the trees. The trees nestled around a small pool fed by a lazy creek. Golden leaves floated on the glassy surface of the water. There was plenty of grass for one horse and enough thick elderberry bushes growing under the trees to hide his fire if he kept it small.

Throwing his right leg over the horn, Dan slid from the saddle. Once on the ground he stretched his long arms and rubbed his back with both hands before turning to remove his mouse-colored mustang's saddle. He took a pair of soft hobbles from his jacket pocket and leaned down to tie them around the pony's slim front legs. Straightening, he unbuckled the neck strap to slide the headstall over the pony's ears and remove the bridle.

He stopped a few minutes to rub the horse's soft nose and ears and scratch some of the damp places on its head where it sweated under the straps of the bridle. Finally, he let the mustang loose to graze on the rank growth of bluestem and gramma that covered the ground in the tiny meadow near the pond.

Gathering up a pile of dry twigs and leaves, Dan built a small fire. When the wood burned down to a bed of red coals, he cooked his supper, and went to bed.

He turned his head toward the sound, straining to hear better. Carefully checking the loads in his pistol, he pulled on his boots and eased out of his blanket. He stood still to listen, holding the weapon ready. He meant to find out what was crying so he could get some sleep. The noise stopped.

Maybe I just imagined it.

Stepping carefully to avoid making noise, Dan moved in the direction he thought the sound came from. He stopped still for a moment, listening. The sound came again.

Someone's crying or I've gone to imagining things.

It was easy for him to follow the sound now. He dropped his pistol back in his holster and walked over to a thick stand of bushes close under a big tree. As he approached the covert the crying sound suddenly became much louder. At the same moment he heard someone speaking softly.

"Please stop crying like that Bryce. Please—please—stop it. You'll just make yourself sick. I know you're hungry, but there's nothing left for you to eat. Go on to sleep now. I'll find us some more food in the morning, I promise I will. Hush your crying now and go on to sleep."

Dan stretched out a long arm to grab a handful of the elderberry bush and shove it to one side. Light from the rising moon revealed the white face of a young boy staring up at him. He looked to be maybe twelve or thirteen years old. The boy held another smaller child cuddled in his arms. Shocked speechless, Dan stared down at the children.

The older child drew back away from Dan, appearing to be more angry than afraid. "You go away and leave us alone, Mister. We ain't hurting anything." The boy's face screwed up in anger or fear. His dark eyes were slits and he almost hissed the words.

Swallowing his astonishment, Dan squatted on his heels to be on a level with the boy's eyes. Striving to keep his voice quiet and calm, he asked, "Who are you, boy? Where're your people? Where's your mother and father?"

"We ain't got no ma, Mister, and our pa ain't here right now." The child's voice trembled a little but still sounded angry. "He told us to wait right here in these bushes until he came back to fetch us. He had to go somewhere on some important business. He said he'd be back before night the same day he left, but it's been three whole days and he ain't come back yet."

Dan shook his head to clear his thoughts. He could hardly believe his eyes or his ears. *How in the world could anybody leave two little children out in the woods alone like this?*

"What's your name, kid?"

The oldest child drew back away from the opening a little, looking to the side as though he was considering running away. His voice got louder, but it continued to tremble. "We ain't got to tell you anything, Mister. You go on now and leave us alone."

"I heard your little brother crying for something to eat. I've got some leftover biscuits and a big can of peaches in my pack. I'd be willing to share with you. Why don't you come on over to my campsite? You're welcome to the food."

"We ain't supposed to move away from this place. Pa told us we had to stay put—right here—exactly where he left us."

"Okay then, stay here. I'll go back over to my camp and bring the food here to you. That way you can stay right where you are. It won't take me a minute."

Thoroughly puzzled, Dan rushed back to his camp and gathered up all the food left in his saddlebags. As he approached the clump of bushes again he felt an instant flash of hope that he'd been dreaming.

Did I really just find two abandoned children? What on earth am I supposed to do with two kids this far away from the Eight?

When he pulled the branches aside again the children

were still there. The older one sat on a blanket and held the little one close. Both stared up at him with wary expressions. Dan reached out and placed his last two biscuits in the older child's hands. He pulled his knife out of his boot, and turned away to cut open the can of peaches. Taking extra care, he cut the top edge of the can smooth enough for the children to drink the peach juice without danger of cutting their lips.

When Dan turned back to hand the older child the can of peaches both biscuits had disappeared. A white crumb glittered in one corner of the littlest child's mouth. The biggest child took the can in both hands to help the little one drink. The fruit and juice disappeared as fast as the biscuits had.

The biggest child kept his dark eyes on Dan's face the whole time. He continued to hold the little one in one arm. They ate so fast that Dan wished he had more food. He couldn't help but think they still looked hungry.

"Have you youngsters got bedrolls or blankets or something to keep you warm? It gets cold as—ah—it gets almighty cold out here at night."

"We've got our blankets and Pa's basket. It's right here beside us."

"What's your name, kid?"

"I'm Anne Marie Gillis, and this here's my brother Bryce."

"Anne Marie? Your name is Anne Marie?" Dan stood up and almost shouted his astonishment. "I—I took you for a boy. I thought you were both boys."

"I ain't a boy." The girl sounded insulted. She held her head up and moved back into the shadows, a little farther away from Dan.

"Well, excuse me all to the dickens, ma'am. You've got on

that cap and jeans and that big old coat. It makes you look like a boy to me. It's kinda dark back in those bushes, too."

"I can't help it if you've got poor eyes."

"Look here, Missy. I don't need your smart mouth."

"I ain't no smart mouth."

"By golly, you sure are a smart mouth."

Dan suddenly realized he was almost shouting at the child. He turned away for a moment, telling himself to calm down.

I can't be standing here arguing with this poor little girl no matter how much of a smart-mouthed brat she is.

He carefully lowered his voice and turned back to question the girl again. "Where'd you youngsters and your pa come from?"

"We used to live down to Wichita, but the dirty old scudder that owned the rooming house we lived in threw us out of our room. We're on our way to New Orleans to live. Pa's got a bunch of kinfolk living there. We're gonna live with them. Least ways, that's where we'll be going as soon as Pa gets back here. He said we're gonna have a big steak and a pair of fine horses to ride after he finishes that important job he agreed to do."

"That sure sounds interesting—is your pa a cattleman?"

"No. Our pa ain't no cattleman. Tending cows is sorry, dirty work and he'd never do it, never in a million years. Cowboys ain't nothing but trash anyway—least that's what Pa says. Our pa worked in the Red Dog Saloon in Wichita. He's the best twenty-one dealer in the state of Kansas. The low-down sucker of a bartender at the Red Dog fired him off his job, that's why we had to move on.

"One of Pa's friends came by our rooming house right when we were packing up to leave town. He paid Pa some money to do a job for him. That's when Pa brought us out here and said he had to hide us in this place."

"What are you supposed to do if he never comes back after you?"

"He is too coming back for us. You can't say that. You're a stupid cowboy." The girl clutched the little boy against her and shrieked the words at Dan. The moon glinted on a tear sliding down her left cheek.

"It's all right, girl. Hush now. Forget I said that. Sure your pa'll come back for you. Don't you start crying now." Her violent reaction to his words made Dan feel miserable.

"I ain't crying."

"Well I can see that plain enough. Look here, girl. I've got to get me some sleep. Can you two manage where you are for the rest of the night?"

The girl's tone changed. Her voice softened and sounded dull, as if she was tired or completely discouraged. Turning her head away from Dan she looked at the ground and asked, "Are you going to go away and leave us here too, Mister?"

Dan almost felt like crying himself. "No—no I'm not going to leave you here. I swear. I'm only going to walk back over yonder where I was trying to sleep before I heard that baby crying. I'm gonna fetch my things over here so I can sleep near you two. I don't think I'd be able to sleep a wink otherwise."

Hurrying back to his campsite, Dan gathered up his possessions. On the second trip he stopped to kick dirt over the remains of his fire. He dropped his saddle and other belongings on a grassy place close to the clump of bushes where the abandoned children lay hidden. Remaking his bed, he stretched out and pulled his blanket up over his shoulders. His head seemed to be spinning.

Exhausted, he finally dropped off to sleep, asking himself, *What should I do with two abandoned children? What on earth should I do with two abandoned kids and one of them a smart-mouthed girl?*

When he looked inside the clump of bushes the next morning the two children were sound asleep. The girl still had one arm around the little boy.

"Wake up you two. I've got some hot water ready and a pinch of tea to flavor it for you. I even found a couple a lumps of sugar you might want. We need to get moving—it's a long ride to where we'll get us the best breakfast in this country."

Anne Marie sat up, rubbing the sleep from her eyes with both hands. She scowled and gave Dan a disgusted look. "We can't leave here with you, Mister. I told you that last night. Pa said that me and Bryce had to stay put, right where we are, no matter what happened. He'll tan my hide for sure when he comes back and sees we've disobeyed him."

"Look girl, you can't stay here any longer, so just forget it. We'll leave your father a message tied to that low limb right over there. I've got some paper and a pencil. I'll tell him exactly where we're going and how he can find you. You youngsters have got to go somewhere where you can get some food and where there'll be somebody to see to your needs."

"I don't need you or anybody else to be seeing to my needs, Mister." The girl yelled, sounding desperate. She stood up and placed her hands on her hips. Dan was surprised to see how tall she was. She wasn't quite as little as he at first thought.

"I can take care of me and Bryce all by myself. You ain't got no call to be messing with us anyway. We ain't bothering you none. You ain't nothing but a stinking, lowdown cattle drover, anyway. I can tell that by the way you're dressed and that saddle of yours. Why don't you just ride on away and leave us alone?"

"Look girl, you shut that smart mouth of yours and get your stuff together. We're leaving here right now."

"I ain't leaving."

"I'll paddle your rear end," Dan shouted, glaring at her.

Anne Marie stared defiantly back at Dan, a fierce expression on her face. She stood with her elbows out and hands on her hips until the little boy woke up. As soon as he sat up and looked around, he started crying for something to eat. She immediately forgot about Dan and reached down to try to shush the child.

When she couldn't convince the boy to stop howling for food, the girl's shoulders drooped as though she had given up. Without another word she knelt to pack up their blankets. She kept her head turned away from Dan the whole time, re- fusing to look at him.

He tied the girl's basket behind his saddle along with his bedroll and saddlebags. Carefully arranging the children's blankets as a pad around and over the horn of his saddle, he made a place for the girl to ride. When he got the blankets settled to his satisfaction he turned to Anne Marie. "Hold tight to your little brother and let me lift you two up here on the front of my saddle."

"I can walk."

"You can't walk as far as we have to go girl, now come here and stop arguing with me about everything."

Dan caught Anne Marie around the waist with both hands and lifted her up in front his saddle. She still held Bryce in her arms. Looking around the little grove, he made sure the note he wrote for Gillis was placed so it could easily be seen. Satisfied he had done all he could to notify the man how to find his children if and when he returned, he climbed into the saddle behind them, wrapping one arm around the girl's middle so she couldn't fall off.

The girl rode without speaking until Dan stopped to open a gate in the Triangle Eight's boundary fence, then she suddenly woke up. Raising her head she began to ask questions as rapidly as she could speak. "Where're you taking us, anyway, Mister? Are you taking us to your own house? Do you have a ma at your house?"

"Why don't you let me answer one of your silly questions before you ask me a couple more?

"Are you kidnapping us?"

"You and your little brother have been abandoned. I'm rescuing you."

"We are not abandoned. I told you that. Pa's going to track you down and shoot you dead for stealing us."

"Hush girl. You're old enough to know that your pa woulda been back after you two kids long before now if he was coming back at all. You couldn't keep staying where you were and you know it. You didn't even have any food left or anything. Anyway, children have got to live with somebody."

The girl ducked her head and stayed quiet for more than five minutes before she spoke again. "Where are you taking us then?"

"To the Triangle Eight. It's a ranch. It's where I work and live. It's been in my family since this whole area belonged to the Indians."

"I never heard of no ranch called the Triangle Eight before. It can't be much."

"You don't know everything, Miss Smarty Pants. The Triangle Eight might not be so much to some people, but it's enough for my family, I'll tell you that. It's where I'm taking you, so why don't you just keep quiet?"

Dan cursed his luck at having to abandon the trail of the stolen cattle and horses, but he knew he had to put the care of two children before chasing a bunch of stolen stock. It didn't matter how he felt about it. The idea that the stock thieves would get away purely riled him, but he knew it couldn't be helped—not at the moment.

It didn't help his mood much when he thought how the ranch foreman, Jack Burton, would fairly split his sides laughing when he saw Dan ride into the ranch yard with two children up on his saddle.

For some reason, Jack always loved to get any kind of joke on me, like he did when I was still about ten years old. Once he got one, he'd ride it into the ground. This one would probably last him a good year.

Henry'll more'n likely throw an out-and-out fit when he sees me. He'll probably stomp around yelling that I shoulda left these two youngsters sit where I found them and kept on trailing the stolen stock.

Dan headed his pony on a beeline for the ranch house.

The route he took would get them there before noon, barring unforeseen problems. He'd be good and hungry by then himself.

His mustang's long trot fairly ate up the miles. By the time the sun got up and had good and warmed them, Anne Marie's head began to droop. The girl gradually relaxed and leaned back against Dan's chest, fast asleep. She still held tight to her brother.

Chapter Two

When Dan rode into the ranch yard Henry came rushing out of the bunkhouse. He literally yanked his body to a stop and stared with his mouth open when he saw the children on Dan's saddle. Finally finding his voice, he yelled, "What in the name of all that's crazy is this? What in the world are you up to now? Who are these boys?"

"They're abandoned children, big brother. I found them hiding in some bushes over to Salt Creek. The oldest one says their pa left them there about three days ago. They were only supposed to stay there for one day until he did some sort of a job and came back for them, but he never did come back. I couldn't leave them there with nobody to care for them. They didn't even have anything left to eat."

"What in the world are you planning to do with them? There's no place here for kids."

Henry Smithson looked enough like his younger brother to be his twin if you didn't look too closely. He had the same black eyes and straight black hair, only he wore his hair pulled back and tied in a single braid that reached below his shoulder blades. He was a couple of inches shorter than Dan, about an inch under six feet tall.

Both wore dark colored jeans and short leather jackets. It was easy to see they were both young, but their faces were burned dark from being outside every day and they were wiry and tough looking from hard work.

"What the heck do you mean there's no place here for youngsters? We were both youngsters not too long ago ourselves and we lived here."

"That's different and you know it. We didn't have any choice."

"Well, neither do these poor little things. They can't live in the woods Henry, and you know it."

"Why in Sam Hill didn't you take them on down to Ma Hainey's? She woulda taken them in."

"I thought of that at first myself, but I can't do that. It's no fit place. The big one here is a girl."

"A girl!" Henry's yell was so loud it awakened Anne Marie.

"Where are we?" she mumbled, looking around at Dan. She jerked her body away from his embrace and yelled, "Get your arm off of me, Mister."

"I only held you up so you and your brother would stay on the horse. You wouldn't want you and your little brother to fall on the ground would you?"

"I ain't going to fall on the ground and neither is Bryce."

"Will you please just shut your yap and hand your brother to Henry so we can get down from this horse?"

"I ain't turning loose of Bryce, Mister, so forget it."

"Hang on tight then. Come over here, Henry. Grab one

side of this ornery critter so I can get her down off this horse."

"Are you telling me this loud-mouth kid is a girl?" Henry reached up and caught Anne Marie's shoulders to help Dan lower both children safely on the ground.

"Oh, drat it all to the devil. The seat of that little kid's britches are sopping wet." Henry wiped his left hand on his jeans and wrinkled up his nose like he smelled something nasty. He turned to stare down at Anne Marie "Don't you have any clean nappies for this kid?"

Anne Marie's face got red, but she held her head high and stared right back. The left side of her jacket and pants were also soaked. "I can't help it, Mister. This kid's just a regular pee pot. He wets on everything, all the time. I don't have any more dry clothes for him, and I ain't had much chance to do any washing lately."

Dan felt bad. It was easy to see the girl felt embarrassed. "Look at your clothes, girl. He's wet all over you. Take this basket of yours and go on in the house there." He pointed to the back door of the house.

"I think I've probably still got some clothes I grew out of that wouldn't be too awful big on you. Let that big boy walk, you don't have to carry him all the time."

"Bryce gets tired walking. He ain't quite four years old."

"Well, he's old enough to make it to the house under his own steam. Set him on his feet and come on with me."

Dan grabbed the basket from the back of his saddle and led the way up the stone walk. Pulling open the screen door, he crossed the back porch to walk into the kitchen of the ranch house. A tiny Latina stood at a stone sink washing some pans. Her shoulders were slightly stooped, and her black hair was full of gray streaks.

The Smithson boys had always called Inez Pretlow aunt, but she was really no formal kin to them. The widow of a man that had served their father as foreman for more than twenty years, she just seemed to be part of the family. When Bill Pretlow died of pneumonia one winter, Inez continued to live in the foreman's house. She really had no place else to go, and the elder Smithson insisted she would have a home on the Triangle Eight as long as she lived.

When Dan and Henry's mother died, Inez started helping in the house. Then when their father died she took over the housekeeping completely. For years she had made it her business to see that Dan and Henry were fed and had clean clothes and a comfortable home.

As Dan led the children into the kitchen, Inez stopped her work and turned to stare, drying her hands on a cloth. "Hola, Danny. Who are these niños?"

"I'll explain later, Tía Inez. Come on with me, you two."

Motioning for the children to follow, he led them straight through the house and down a long hall to the second room on the left. Grabbing the knob he pulled the door wide open and waved the children in ahead of him.

"This is my bedroom. I'll move my things out to the bunkhouse and you two can stay in here."

Anne Marie picked Bryce up again and held him against her chest. Her eyes filled with fear and she almost screamed her panic. "I ain't staying in this place and you can't make me. Pa'll never be able to find us here. You can't keep us. It ain't right."

"Stop yelling, girl, for goodness sake. I'm getting sick and tired of your mouth. You saw me tie a note on that clump of bushes you two were hiding behind. If your Pa comes back to that place, he'll know exactly where to find you."

Dan placed the girl's basket on his bed and asked, "Do you have any clean clothes in this basket?"

"No we don't. I already told you we didn't have no more clean clothes. Don't you listen when people talk?"

"Look brat. I'm trying to help you. I don't appreciate your attitude."

"Why don't you just take us back where you found us and leave us alone then?"

"Because no adult can leave two little children sitting in the bushes ten miles from nowhere. It's a rule, and everybody's got to live by it. Your fool pa had no business leaving you alone in such a place, anyway—you know that as well as I do. You're also big enough to know that something bad must have happened to your pa to keep him from coming back for you youngsters."

"I know." Anne Marie dropped her head. Her voice softened to a flat whisper. "Pa would've been back long ago if he could. His spare bottle of medicine is in that basket along with his papers."

The expression on the girl's face was serious. Dan stared at her a moment, wondering if she meant to sound so grown up and bitter. He decided he was going to open that basket and have a look. He hoped it would have something in it to help him figure out where the children belonged.

Unbuckling the belt holding the wicker lid down tight, Dan pulled the basket open. At first it looked to be full of clothes—clothes that smelled like they were badly in need of a wash. He removed the clothes and dropped them on the floor. Once they were gone he found a large family bible, two packets of papers wrapped in oilcloth, a woman's picture in an ornate frame and underneath everything, a quart jar of whiskey. Dropping whiskey on the bed, he carefully returned the other things to the basket.

"I'm going to put this basket on the shelf in my closet. It looks like some of these papers could be real important. They'll be safe in here."

Anne Marie didn't yell, but she still watched him with angry eyes. "You give that basket back to me, Mister. You can't take our things."

"Will you please calm down, girl? I'm not taking a thing of yours except this jar of brown whiskey. You kids sure don't need it. Your stinking basket is safe right here on this shelf, see it? You're gonna be staying in this room so you can get it any time you want.

"Speaking of stinking, you two strip off and add those filthy clothes of yours to this pile of dirty things on the floor. I'll send Tía Inez in here with warm water for you to clean yourselves up some. You'll find plenty of towels in the top drawer of that big maple chest over there."

"I ain't taking my clothes off."

"You'll take your clothes off, Missy, or somebody'll take them off for you. Tía Inez'll help you clean up the little boy. You just stop your grousing and get busy."

Grabbing the jar of whiskey from the bed, Dan left the room, slamming the door. He strode down the hall to the kitchen, unsure whether to be angry or amused.

When he reached the kitchen door he said, "Tía Inez, please put some hot water in the washtub. I'll help you carry it back to my room. When we get that done I'll go get some buckets of cool water to make a good bath. The little boy ran out of nappies and both of those two smell to high heaven.

"You'll have to figure out something for them to wear until their clothes can be washed and dried. They sure can't wear the things they've got on anymore. They stink so bad they'd knock a buzzard off a manure wagon."

"Who are these niños, Danny? Where did they come from?"

"It's a real puzzle to me, Tía. I found them hiding under a bunch of bushes beside that little branch that runs off of Salt Creek. It's just down that long hill past the county road. I set out to follow some stock that got stolen and night caught me over there. I made me a camp, ate my supper and turned in for the night. I'd almost gone to sleep when I heard the littlest one crying. I followed the sound and there sat those children, hiding in a clump of elderberry bushes. I could hardly believe my eyes at first. The girl says their pa left them there and told them not to move. She swears he promised to come back for them the next day, but he never showed up."

"One is a girl?"

"I know it's hard to tell with her bundled up in that big coat, but the big one's a girl, believe it or not. She said her name's Anne Marie. The little one is her brother, she calls him Bryce."

"Pobrecitas."

"Yeah, you're right about that. They're poor little things, without a doubt. If you'll get 'em clean and fed I'd sure appreciate it. They're probably about to starve right now. They were hungry last night and all I had for them to eat was two cold biscuits and a can of peaches. All I could give 'em for breakfast was some warm tea with a little bit of sugar I found in the bottom of my kit.

"I'll help you with the water, then I'm going to get me a good night's sleep. When I get up tomorrow I've got to try to find the trail of the kid's pa. I don't know anything, of course, but I been thinking that it's right much of a coincidence that that man left those kids right where he did. I mean—they were doggone close to where somebody flattened a section of Triangle Eight fence and drove off a good-sized bunch of our stock."

A concerned expression on her face, Inez dipped hot water from the reservoir of the wood stove into the tin washtub. When she finished and put the dipper away, Dan helped her carry the tub to the bedroom. Both children were still dressed, sitting on the floor. Anne Marie held the sleeping Bryce in her arms and leaned back against the side of the bed. She looked almost asleep herself.

She lifted her head and stared first at the tub of steaming water and then at Dan. "I ain't washing in no tub and you can't make me."

Dan looked across the tub at Inez and shook his head.

"Go on outside and get me two buckets of cool water, Daniel," Inez said. "I will take care of these children."

Relieved, Dan left the room to get the water. Henry stood in the middle of the kitchen with his hands on his hips. "Have you lost your mind, boy? We can't be taking care of two kids. We've got too much work to do. You should have taken them on to town or someplace."

"I don't see why we can't take care of them. Tía Inez is here, she'll help us."

"She doesn't sleep in the house. It's one thing for you to

give up your bed and move out to the bunkhouse if that's what you want to do. But I don't want to give up my room for some strange kids. Especially when one of them is that bratty, big-mouthed girl. If she stays here I'll have to sleep in the bunkhouse too. It's plain to see she's too old for me to be sleeping in the house with her in the other room unless Tía Inez sleeps here at night."

"Henry, please calm yourself down. Tía Inez'll sleep in the house as long as we need her and you know it. You won't have to give up your room. I can sleep in the bunkhouse for a few days while I find out where these youngsters belong. It won't kill you or me either. I'll figure this out as soon as I can.

"Right now I've got to go pump some cold water for their bath. But I'm going to ride back over there to the spot where I found them as soon as I wake up tomorrow morning and try to pick up the trail of those rustlers again. I think the man that left those youngsters in the bushes might be mixed up in driving off that bunch of stock."

"What do you mean about rustlers? What happened? What stock are you talking about?"

"Somebody downed about eight sections of fence over near that little chert hill we used to call a castle, and drove out a bunch of cows and maybe eight or ten of our horses."

"When in Sam Hill were you planning on telling me about it?"

"How about . . . I'm telling you about it right now?"

"Could you track 'em—could you tell where they were headed?"

"They started out headed to the west and turned north. I figured they'd turn due west when they reached the main road, but they kept on going straight across the road to the north. I'm not exactly sure what they're doing, but I figure I can probably catch up with them in a couple of days if I push it."

"Do you really think you can follow the trail now?" Henry stepped back a little so he didn't have to look up into Dan's eyes.

"It ain't rained any. I shouldn't have any trouble following a bunch of stock that big. I also think I might find some interesting tracks leaving the place where those youngsters were hiding. I believe their pa mighta left them there so he could join up with the rustlers. If that's what he was really doing out there, I don't know."

"I can't believe you didn't tell me this when you first came in."

Come on, Henry," Dan said. "Quit arguing and let me get finished with this so I can get some sleep."

"Oh, all right then. I'll go tell Inez what we're doing and ask her to sleep in Dad's room for a few nights to be near the brats."

Streaks of red and pink decorated the gray sky as Dan left the ranch yard the next morning. He rode a fresh horse and Inez handed him a bundle of extra food and a second canteen. It added up that he might be out several days on this trip, maybe as long as a week, so he wanted to be prepared. Urging his horse to a mile-eating trot, he took a direct route back to the place where he left the trail.

It took more than an hour of careful study of the ground around the group of trees where he discovered the children to find the right tracks. Starting near the place where the children had hidden, Dan rode around the little patch of trees in ever-widening circles. He was almost ready to give up when he spotted tracks leading away from the area. He followed them only a few yards before they joined the trail of the stolen cattle and horses. There was no way to tell whether the horse's tracks actually joined the herd or were made earlier and simply covered by the passing of the cattle and horses.

Dan felt pleased that he'd been able to identify the tracks of the horse ridden by the man who left the children in the grove. And that he'd be able to identify them if he ever saw them again. The shoe on the horse's left front foot had a cross bar that ran from one side to the other. Most likely the hoof had split at some time and the shoe was specially made with that bar to hold it together while it healed.

Wishing someone rode with him who could check the far side of the trail left by the cattle, Dan continued to follow the herd, riding on the south side of the tracks. He knew the man he looked for might leave the trail somewhere and it worried him that the tracks left by the herd covered a space too wide for him to watch but one side at a time.

The land he rode over was similar to most of Triangle Eight, rolling and generally well watered. Grass grew tall and thick in most places. He noticed thick clumps of trees every few miles. Twice he saw deer in the distance, much too far away to get a shot.

Making dry camp in a group of pin oaks that night, Dan used most of the water in the second canteen for his horse. He reminded himself that he'd have to find water the next day. "It shouldn't be hard. Water is plentiful around here this time of year."

In the morning of the third day on the trail Dan began to smell dust. He knew the smell indicated that someone, probably as many as two or three people, or a group of cattle or horses, moved nearby. Topping a small rise, he stopped to study the area. Nothing moved within his sight.

Riding at a smooth easy pace, he wasn't tired, so he decided to keep moving instead of stopping for a noonday break. The smell of dust made him uneasy and if someone else was in the area he wanted to be mounted and alert when they showed up.

The camping place he chose that night showed recent use. It lay near a large spring that was almost hidden in a grove of sycamore trees. Saving his other supplies, Dan made his second meal out of some of the bread and sliced beef Inez packed in his saddlebag, and didn't bother with a fire. Tired out, he unrolled his bed on the thick grass. Removing his boots and wrapping up in his blanket, he fell asleep in minutes.

It was getting close to morning when Dan woke up. The moon had set and the sky was that strange painted-looking gray color it takes on just before dawn. A horse moved somewhere in the clump of trees. Dan looked around. His horse was directly in his sight, standing still.

When he heard the jingle of metal, Dan sat up to listen, his pistol in his hand. The light was so poor it was impossible to see anything more than a few feet away, but he could tell from the sounds that another horse was nearby.

Easing out of his blankets, he pulled on his boots and moved closer to the trunk of a big tree, holding his gun ready. He could hear the horse's hooves as they hit the hard ground close to the spring. After a moment or two he could see the animal. As it came closer he noticed that it wore a saddle and bridle, but had no rider.

Dan kept his gun in his hand and waited. He looked around the clearing and listened carefully but couldn't see or hear anyone. Finally, he left the tree and eased closer to the horse. He approached it directly, watching on either side in case someone followed. He couldn't see far in the gloom, but finally satisfied that no one was with the horse, he reached out and caught its bridle.

A wet nose touched his shoulder. The horse had been to the spring to drink. He patted its nose and worked around to its side, putting one hand on the saddle. The leather was cold. No one had been in the saddle for a long time.

"Easy boy, easy now—come on here. I've got a little bag of oats in my saddlebag. Let's take that bit out of your mouth so you can eat. Hold on a minute."

Darting his eyes from side to side and watching every shadow, Dan slipped his gun in the waist of his jeans to keep it handy while he fed the horse two handfuls of the oats. Rigging another pair of hobbles out of a piece of rope, he led the tall bay over near his pony and removed its saddle. Dropping the gear near his bed, he resolved to examine it carefully as soon as it was light enough to see properly.

Taking his Colt in his left hand again he moved silently into the trees and slowly searched the wooded area. After more than fifteen minutes of creeping from tree to tree, circling the grove, he finally convinced himself that he would not find the horse's rider.

Returning to camp, Dan stopped to watch the tall gelding as it grazed near his pony. It seemed to be glad of the other horse's company. He shook his head in puzzlement and returned to his blankets, hoping to get at least another hour of sleep before full light.

What a strange thing to happen. Where in heck could this horse's rider have gotten to? No rider and a saddled horse walking around in the middle of the night—that's downright scary if you ask me.

Dan tossed and turned, his gun near his hand, until he finally dropped off to sleep again. The sun had moved above the trees when he woke up. Disgusted with himself for sleeping so long, he skipped a fire and chewed some jerky for breakfast so he could get moving. He couldn't stop thinking that he might have been truly lucky he didn't light a fire the night before.

When his horse was ready to go he rearranged the loose bridle and saddle on his night visitor. In daylight he could see that the horse was a handsome blood bay, long-legged and sleek. He looked well fed and was obviously well trained, allowing Dan to manage him easily.

Leading the extra horse by its reins, Dan rode to the northwest, back on the trail of the herd. He had a feeling he'd better be ready for anything. Loosening his Winchester in its sheath, he leaned forward on his mount's neck every time he crested a hill to avoid making too easy a target in case someone was laying for him. He was gaining fast on the Triangle Eight horses and cattle. The tracks looked to be no more than a day old.

Whoever the people are behind the herd, they seem to think no one could possibly be following them. Maybe they're just outlaws—not cowhands—and really don't know ranchers patrol their fences on a regular schedule. That might help explain why they didn't have wire cutters with them, too. They probably think they've got days or maybe even weeks before anybody finds out the stock's been stolen.

It was almost noon when he spotted the buzzards. They looked like black dots moving against a fluffy white cloud when he first saw them. He watched as they flew lower to skim the top of a patch of cottonwoods, then whirl in circles and come back down to land in the top limbs of the tallest trees. Uneasy, he lifted his reins and urged his horse to a canter, still holding the lead on the extra horse.

It took Dan almost an hour to reach the grove of trees. Five or six of the buzzards flew up high and hovered in the air over the trees as he came close. Several of the ugly birds stayed where they were, perched in the top of the tall trees, unafraid—waiting for their meal.

A man lay face down on the ground in a small meadow. The buzzards hadn't touched him yet. Dismounting, Dan tied the reins of the extra horse to his saddle and dropped his horse's reins on the grass, glad he'd trained every horse in his string to stand ground hitched.

Dan stood close to the horses and took time to check the area carefully before he moved toward the body. He took his rifle from the saddle sheath and cocked it. Holding the weapon ready, he moved closer to the body.

A sweetish smell filled the air. It was hard for him to breathe. He knew the smell meant that the man had been dead for at least several hours, probably more than a day. When he stepped closer to the body he could see a small hole with black streaks around it in the back of the man's dark green frock coat.

Pulling his bandanna up over his nose to make it easier to breathe, Dan knelt beside the man and checked his pockets, looking for something to identify him. The pockets he could reach held a worn deck of cards and nothing else. He grasped the man by one shoulder and pulled to turn him over. The body was limp. The stiffening of the body after death was over, confirming his idea that the man had been dead at least a day, if not more.

A letter stuck out of the man's shirt pocket. Dan eased the paper out and unfolded it. It was addressed to Raoul Gillis. "Well of all the hard luck. This man is likely Anne Marie and Bryce's pa."

Dan sat back on his boot heels and examined the man's face. Even in death he was handsome in a brutish sort of way. His face was broad and his cheekbones were prominent. There was a noticeable bump on one side of his prominent nose. It looked like his nose may have been broken in a fight at sometime. His hair hung straight almost to his shoulders and was coal black.

This fella's hair is exactly the same as those children's, but if this man was their pa they sure didn't take after him any in their looks.

Standing up, Dan slid the letter into his inside jacket pocket and returned to his horse. Untying his bedroll, he removed the ground sheet. He rerolled the blankets and tied them back behind his saddle. Spreading the ground sheet out, he wrapped it around the body. It was a struggle, and he had to tie the horse's head to a tree to make him stand still for it, but he finally wrestled the dead man up on the back of the big bay and draped him across the saddle. He took a rope from the bay's saddle and tied the body securely in place.

Leaving the trail of the stolen cattle at the next water hole, Dan turned to ride back south and east to a little settlement on the main branch of Salt Creek called Severy City. It wasn't far. He set the horses to a trot and in about an hour he spotted the top of the buildings as he skirted around the edge of High Lonesome Hill. There was no sheriff or lawman in the little town, so he asked at the store for a piece of paper and pencil so he could write out what happened for the U.S. Marshal.

Dan paid the town's preacher to take care of burying the body and notifying the authorities. Leaving the bay horse at the livery, he didn't stay for the burial. After he refilled his canteens and bought some more jerky and a loaf of bread, he headed back to the trail. He had left his own horse at the livery along with the bay and rode a big black with a white star on his forehead. The horse was a loan from Stewert, the owner of the livery and an old friend of his father's. He hurried northwest, anxious to get back on the trail of the stolen stock.

The dead man and the trip to the settlement cost him almost four hours, but when he got back to the trail, Dan could tell that he was still less than two days behind the herd. Whoever the thieves were, they evidently thought they were out of reach of any pursuit. They were giving the cattle time to graze as they moved along. Their trail led due west now—headed straight for Wichita and the cattle market.

Pushing his new mount hard the rest of that day and the next, Dan stopped a little before dark the second night. He could hear the sounds of cattle in the distance. Refilling both of his canteens, he watered his horse at a little creek. Loosening the saddle and removing the bit from its mouth, he hobbled the black and left it to graze. Using a small tree branch as a broom, he cleared the rocks and twigs from a spot beside a big tree to sit back and rest.

He planned to wait for moonrise, then go after the

rustlers. When the moon gave enough light so he could see to walk without making too much noise, Dan stood up and stretched the kinks out of his back. Checking his rifle and handgun, he started walking toward the sound of the cattle, leaving the pony grazing contentedly.

Chapter Three

It took Dan a full ten minutes of fast walking to reach the edge of the herd. As he approached he could see the glow of a campfire over to his left, close under a small grove of black jack oaks. The cattle grazed quietly, spread out over several acres. He stood still to count the ones he could see. He could see more than fifty.

The stolen horses stood close together in the edge of the trees. As he crept nearer he could see that they wore rope hackamores and were bunched in a rope corral. He counted twelve, more than he thought. Three other horses wearing rope hobbles grazed between the cattle and the grove of trees.

"I'm going to bet that means there's only three of the low-down rustling sidewinders chasing our stock," Dan whispered softly.

Removing the rawhide loop that held his pistol tight in its holster and cocking his rifle, Dan eased across the open and into the dark area under the trees, careful to move as quietly as he could. As he worked his way nearer the glow of the fire, he used his toes to test the ground for twigs before he made a step.

One of the men sat up beside the campfire. His shoulders rested against an old stump. His head drooped and his chin touched his chest as though he was dozing.

Moving carefully as he circled around to the other side of the campfire, Dan reached a position where he could see the side of the man's face.

He's not just dozing—I think he's sound asleep.

Two other men snored loudly. They lay on the ground with their feet close to the fire, rolled in blankets.

When he reached a spot directly in front of the man leaning back against the stump, Dan could see that his eyes were closed and his mouth hung open. As Dan had guessed, the man was sound asleep; his body looked limp and his legs were folded under his body. The butt of his pistol showed in his holster. A new looking Winchester rifle lay across his knees, but his limp hands had slipped down to lie relaxed on the ground beside him. They were at least a foot away from the weapon.

Turning over in his mind several ways he might be able to grab the rustler's gun, Dan finally decided there was nothing for it, all he could do was charge in there ready to shoot. He couldn't see any way to avoid a fight. With all three men asleep, he'd have the advantage. Leaving his rifle on the ground he stood up straight, drew his Colt, and stepped out into the glow of the campfire.

"Wake up boys," he yelled. "It's time to pay the piper."

The man sleeping against the stump started up so violently he knocked his rifle off his knees and beyond his grasp. The gun almost landed in the campfire. He struggled to his feet yelling obscenities and lunged for his handgun. Dan's bullet caught him in the face and knocked him back against the stump. His body flipped backward and slid to the ground, his gun still in his holster. The two men on the ground didn't make a sound. Untangling themselves from their blankets, they stood up slowly, holding their hands in the air and watching Dan warily.

Using their own ropes, Dan tied their wrists and ankles. When he finished, he wrapped the end of the ropes around a nearby tree and tied it securely. He went back to the fire and grabbed the dead man by the front of his shirt to drag him away from the glow of the fire. Kicking dirt over the blood that stained the ground, he sat down by the fire.

The two rustlers watched without speaking as Dan sloshed water around in a cup that was sitting near the fire. When he decided the cup was clean enough for him to drink from, he filled it with coffee and sat back against the tree to look the men over.

"You boys just settle yourselves down, now. You'll be all right, although you may be a little stiff in the morning from being tied up like that. I'll be taking you over to the settlement early tomorrow. The U.S. Marshal should be getting in there around about midday. He'll take good care of you.

"The marshal's coming to take a report on a dead fella I took in there a couple a days ago. It's a funny thing about that. I found that man's body on your back trail. He died about four days back, I'd guess. You two wouldn't happen to know how that fella came to be shot in the back, would you?"

Neither man answered. They simply stared at Dan.

"If you two can't talk, you might as well go on back to

sleep. We're not going anywhere until sunup anyway." Dan looked from one man to the other. "Don't go trying anything, either. I'm gonna keep this six-gun pointed right at your heads for the rest of the night."

After he made sure the horses were safely settled for the night, Dan returned to sit by the fire. Tired from days of hard riding and little rest, he fought sleep, but no matter how hard he tried to keep his eyes open, he dozed off and on until the eastern sky began to lighten.

Thankful the night was finally over he stood up to stretch and stirred up the fire, adding more wood. When the new wood burned down to a bed of coals, he found the rustlers' food supplies, made a fresh pot of coffee, and cooked a pan of bacon.

One of the tied up rustlers looked to be about fifteen. He watched hungrily as Dan cooked the bacon. When he saw Dan begin to eat the bacon right out of the pan the boy asked, "Ain't you going to fix us no food to eat, Mister?"

Dan laughed out loud. "You fellas'll get fed in town. Just tell the marshal you're hungry. I'm not bothered about waiting on you."

"Them's our vittles you're making so free with."

"Yes, and those cows and horses you sneaking varmints meant to steal belong to me and my brother. You boys not only cost me days for tracking you, you made me a mountain a work putting that stretch of fence you knocked down back in shape. And if that ain't enough, you saddled me with two youngsters when you killed that fella I found dead in that little tangle of cottonwoods a few miles back along your trail."

The older rustler just stared at Dan with a look of hatred, but the boy argued, "We ain't none of us shot no fella along the trail. We ain't seen no kids nowhere around here either, I swear we ain't."

"I figured you'd say that. But it still looks like right much of a coincidence for that man to be lying dead right there on your back trail. To my way of thinking, it just stands to reason that you fellas had something to do with his killing."

"Well, reason or not, we ain't shot nobody."

Dan ignored the boy and sat by the fire sipping coffee and thinking about what happened. He wondered if perhaps the U.S. Marshal would find a way to be a little easier on one of the rustlers if he was willing to tell him something to clear up the mystery of Gillis' killing.

He figured the boy might even be younger than he looked. He sort of hated to see anybody that young get sent to prison for rustling. He stared at the boy, wondering what kind of man he might make if he the marshal would give him a chance.

When Dan didn't say anything else, the boy continued, "We didn't have no other guy with us at all, Mister. It wasn't nobody but Pete here and old Red, what you killed last night, and me, I swear to it. Warn't no other fella with us and we ain't killed nobody."

"I still say it's an awful big coincidence for that man to be lying there dead when you fellas passed to the south of that patch of woods no more that a few hours before I found his body. If you could see your way clear to unravel the mystery of that killing, I'll bet the marshal would go a little easier on you."

"I think maybe I seen that little patch of woods you spoke about when we passed through there. We saw two dudes riding up there, too. It happened two or three days ago at least.

Those fellas were at too much of a distance for us to see their faces to know them, but they were near enough for us to see that they were both dressed up pretty fancy."

"I found the dead man in that patch of cottonwood trees where there's a little trickle of a creek fed by a spring," Dan said. "Is that where you mean?"

"That's shore the place I mean, Mister. One of them fellas rode a big blood-bay horse and the other had him a grulla. They was way too far off for us to tell who they was."

The other rustler yelled at the boy, "Will you shut your flapping mouth, Simon Kendry? Nobody's gonna get any marshal to go easier on you, least of all this lowdown murderer. You've always been backward and now you're acting plumb stupid. This here man's just talking to get what he can out of you. Don't be such a sap."

Dan left the bound man and boy yelling back and forth at each other and walked over to catch up their horses. Leading two of the rustler's horses close to the men, he untied the legs of the older man, helped him mount the horse and tied his hands to the saddle horn.

He had to poke the rustler in the back with his Colt and threaten to knock him on his head with the pistol three different times before he would hold still, but he finally got his legs tied together under the horse's belly. Tying a piece of rope on one of the boy's legs before he helped him up on his horse made it easier for Dan to reach under the horse's belly and tie his legs together without a fight.

Once the men were settled on their horses and securely tied, Dan attached their horse's reins to a long piece of rope and led them with him as he worked. Wrapping the dead rustler in a blanket, he wrestled his body up on one of the horses. Finally, he mounted one of the extra horses bareback and led them all back to where he left his own horse.

Still holding the rope on the rustler's horses, he awkwardly got his own horse ready to ride and tied the one he'd been riding back on the rope with the others. Leading two men tied on horses and another carrying the body, Dan entered the settlement at the exact same time as the marshal. Dan thankfully turned the two rustlers and the body of their partner over to him.

"These three men knocked down a fence and run off about fifty or sixty head of Triangle Eight cows and twelve of our horses, Marshal Jenks. I tracked them down. When I tried to take 'em prisoner I had to shoot this one here."

The marshal looked nearly worn out. He was a small man with wispy strands of dull gray hair showing under his floppy black hat. His blue eyes looked washed out in his weather-beaten, sun-browned face. Dan figured him for close to fifty years old.

"You're the youngest Smithson boy, ain't you, son?" The marshal turned his head to spit tobacco as he waited for Dan to answer.

"I'm Daniel Smithson," he said.

"I knowed your pa and your grandpa. They were both fine men. They were hard as nails, I know for a fact, but salt of the earth. They come into this country as some of the first settlers. Where's your brother Henry? Did you track these men alone?"

"Henry's over at home, getting ready for the roundup, Marshal. It didn't take no posse to track down these fools."

"Don't go getting your back up now, son. It's just a little

unusual for dead bodies to be showing up so close together—makes me kinda nervous."

"I explained everything about that other fella I brought in here to that preacher. I left him a letter to give you, too."

"Well, how about you taking yourself a little rest while I go find that preacher. I'll get his story and read the letter, then you and me'll have us a talk."

"I'm not willing too wait long, Marshal. I've got a herd of cows and twelve horses to get back over to the Eight."

"You can wait an hour." Jenk's voice had a hard edge.

Dan's voice sounded as hard as the marshal's did. "As long as it's no more than that."

Dismounting in front of Coleman's mercantile, Dan tied his horse to the rail. He went inside and bought some cheese and crackers and a bottle of small beer. Returning to the porch, he sat on the edge with his legs dangling down to eat while he waited. It wasn't more than ten minutes before the marshal rode back up the street and joined him.

"I reckon you did everything as right as you could be expected to, son. The preacher explained to me what you told him, including all about those children. I'll rent a rig and ride along back to your ranch as soon as I can get rid of these prisoners. If you'll see to those youngsters for a few more days I'll pick them up then. I can drive them right on over to Wichita to the orphanage."

A wave of resentment flowed over Dan. His face turned red as he said, "You mean to tell me that you don't plan to do anything to try to find their people? I left that letter for you. That ought to tell you something about where to look."

"Did you read that letter, sonny?"

"No, I didn't read the letter. It wasn't addressed to me."

"Well, excuse me all to the devil. I thought you were interested in those children."

"I am interested in them, of course I am. But I turned that letter over to you because I thought you'd try to find their people, not up and throw the poor little kids in some dog-gone orphanage."

"You make it sound like the orphanage is a prison or something like."

"Well it ain't much better and you well know it. You can just forget all about that, right now. Henry and me'll raise those children ourselves if we can't find their people. I'm not seeing them thrown in no blasted orphanage."

"Calm yourself down, sonny. Let's us go get that letter and read it. I left it over at the preacher's house. It might have something in it to tell where some of those youngsters' people are. Leave those fellas tied on their horses. I'll get the preacher to bury the dead one and lead the others on down to Coffeyville where they've got a place I can lock them up."

"Marshal, I've got to hurry up and hire me a couple of men to go get my stock that those sorry, lowdown snakes were trying to run off. I set out after them by myself because I only expected to find out who it was that was doing the raiding. I didn't figure on trying to get the stock back without any help. I reckoned on getting me some men to help before I faced the rustlers, but they made it so easy I guess I sorta got carried away."

"You sure did at that. I think there's a bounty on that ranny you shot in the face. He had some letters on him that gave his name. Seems to me like I can remember seeing that name on a flyer sometime recently. There oughta be something going on that ugly piece of work the young'un calls Pete, too."

"If it is, you send the money on out to the Triangle Eight, and I'll set it aside for those two youngsters. If we can't find their people they're gonna need something behind them."

"That's a thoughtful thing, son. Hold on a minute there, here comes that preacher. Let me get him started burying those fellas, and I'll get that letter for you."

The letter was written on heavy, embossed paper and addressed to Raoul Gillis at an address on Douglas Avenue in Wichita. It was postmarked in St. Louis. Dan unfolded the letter and read it through. "This letter is signed by a man that has the same name as the one the girl calls herself. But Marshal, that girl doesn't talk like she's been raised up by educated people. She speaks like she's been around somebody with no education at all."

"I don't know what to think about that, son. This letter's addressed to some fella called Gillis but it's sure as heck written and signed by an educated man. The best I can make out of that scratched up signature is Andrew Devereaux. Look at that handwriting, will you? It's a puzzle."

"I remember the name that was on the outside of this letter, and that place, Château d'Arc. That's a French sounding name, Marshal, so I think that first name must be André, not Andrew. It's a fact those kids look as French as any of those Canadians that live over in Fall River. I'll give them that—but the girl shore don't sound it when she talks."

"Where's this Château Dark?"

"I'm sure I don't know," Dan shook his head. "The letter came from St. Louis, but the girl said something about going to New Orleans to live with her pa's kinfolk. Maybe that's where it is. It makes better sense to me than St. Louis."

"From what this letter says, I figure the fella that wrote it was paying somebody to keep those children. It was most likely the dead man you brought in here. The one that had the letter in his pocket."

"Yeah, that's likely it. I figured he was probably their pa."

"If he really was their pa."

"You know, you might have something there," Dan said, "I think it could be that fella was the man those kids called pa. Whether he really was their pa is a mystery to me. Those kids have got a bunch of papers and a family bible with them, though. I'll get me a good look at 'em when I get back to the ranch. They might clear this up for us."

"What about the other man those two rustlers claimed they saw riding along with the dead man?"

"I can't figure out how he fits in, unless he's the one who actually shot that Gillis fella in the back." Dan shook his head.

"Maybe we'll find out. If that was the man who killed those kids' pa or the man that was going as their pa, he might be out looking for them. I figure you and Henry better be extra watchful for a while. It's a chance he might come after you."

"We'll be careful. If you're satisfied, Marshal, I'll go find me some riders and get that stock started on the road toward home. Maybe while I'm doing it I can figure out something about who those youngsters really are."

"Take care of yourself, son. I'll be over to the Triangle Eight in a few days."

Dan waved his hand at the marshal as he turned to go back inside the store. He approached Coleman to ask, "Do you have any idea where I might find a couple of hard working men to help me move a bunch of stock?"

"I don't know for sure, but it seems like there's always some men standing around town doing nothing. Why don't you try asking a couple of those fellas sitting out on my porch."

Stepping back outside, Dan turned to face four men who sat in straight back chairs leaning back against the front wall of the store building. He had nodded to the men when he entered the store, but paid little attention to them.

"Howdy, fellas. I'm looking for a couple of drovers to move about fifty head of stock back over to the Triangle Eight. I figure it'll be about four days' hard work. I'll pay cash money, two dollars a day a man."

The man sitting closest to Dan stood up quickly. He looked about grown, but Dan thought he probably wasn't over about sixteen.

"That sounds interesting to me, Mister," he said, "I'm Joe Slade. This is my brother Paul." He turned to wave his hand to the boy who sat next to him. "We need some work, and we'll work hard."

The other boy stood up. He looked even younger than his brother did. Dan couldn't imagine that either one was much more than fifteen or sixteen years old.

"You fellas look mighty young."

"We've got good horses and we know how to work cattle. We'll work hard, Mister. We need the work."

An older man stood up and walked closer to grab the first boy's shoulder and push him aside. "Get on out of here, Slade. There's men around here that might want a couple a days work. This rancher don't want no half-breed boys working his cattle. He'd be afraid you two'd be busy stealing his stock instead of helping him move his cows to where he wants them."

"I'm Brady, Mister," the man said, turning to Dan. "I can help you find some good drovers. All three of the Johnston boys are over to the saloon right now. They come to town looking for a way to earn them some cash money. They'd make you good hands."

Dan straightened to his full height and stared down at the older man. "I was talking to Mr. Slade here, if you don't mind, Brady. I don't think I'll be needing your help, and I sure don't want any help from the Johnston brothers."

"What the devil do you mean by that? You some kind of Indian lover?" Brady screwed up his face and scowled at Dan. He moved closer, and the stench of his breath almost gave Dan the heaves.

"What I mean, Brady, is you should go on about your own business and leave mine alone." Dan stepped back to the edge of the porch, away from the man's stench.

Brady turned to slip off his jacket and throw it on a nearby chair. "What are you trying to do, sonny, get out of my reach?"

"I'm not concerned about you in the least, except that you smell like dead fish soaked in alcohol."

"Why, you scrawny, no-count cow-chaser, I'll knock you into the middle of next week."

Watching the man's hands, Dan took another step back and jumped from the porch to the dirt road. Moving away from the horses, he stood with his hands on his hips and looked back up at the man. "If you're so anxious to knock somebody around, Brady, come on out here and I'll feed you some dirt."

His face flaming, Brady fairly roared in anger as he jumped from the side of the porch. Fists high, he dashed into the street and ran toward Dan. Leaping sideways and sticking out one foot, Dan kicked Brady on his ankle as he rushed past him. He stepped back and laughed aloud as the man slid on his belly through a fresh pile of horse apples.

Brady got to his feet and wiped himself off. Lowering his head he lunged at Dan again. His fist slid over Dan's shoulder and scraped his right ear. Dan slammed his left fist into the side of the larger man's neck and jumped back out of his reach.

It was obvious to Dan that if the brute ever got a good grip on him he was a goner. Brady probably outweighed him by fifty pounds. His only advantage was his quickness. Holding his fists high, he charged. Slamming a left followed swiftly by a right to the man's stomach, Dan ducked back out of reach of a vicious swipe of Brady's huge right hand. Brady charged in close and caught Dan with a wicked overhand right just over his left eye.

Groggy, Dan staggered back and to the side, barely avoiding Brady's follow-up swing. Shaking his head to clear it, he took several steps to the right, blocked Brady's left and hit him in the body again with his right. Again, Brady moved in to land a staggering left over Dan's eye. Blood started flowing. Dan backed away, and Brady rushed in, knocking Dan to the dirt with a smashing right.

When Dan hit the ground his Colt flew out of his holster and landed at Brady's feet. When Brady spotted the pistol lying out of Dan's reach in the dirt, he grinned. Placing one foot on Dan's gun he slammed his hand to his hip and pulled his own handgun.

Just as Brady brought the gun level with Dan's head Marshal Jenks yelled, "Drop it or you die right where you are, Mister."

Brady's whole body jerked in surprise. He turned to face Jenks, dropping his hand to let his pistol hang straight down beside his leg. He glared at the marshal for a moment and then looked back down at his weapon. Without a word he holstered the pistol and turned on his heel to stomp off down the street.

Dan stood up and brushed himself off. Turning to Jenks he said, "I reckon you saved my life, Marshal." Holding his hand against his bleeding forehead he continued, "It didn't look like that fella was going to wait to give me a fair break with that handgun."

Marshal Jenks nodded grimly as he returned his own gun to his holster. "You've got that right, son. Pick up your weapon and let's go see if there's anybody around here to help you stop that cut from bleeding."

Dan untied his bandanna, and pressed it against his eyebrow. "Gosh, I wondered why I was having so much trouble seeing."

"Whew," Joe Slade said, still standing on the porch. "I thought for sure there'd be a killing right here in front of us, and neither Paul or me are carrying a gun. That fella was Ben Brady. He claims to be some sort of a gunfighter."

"Well, I ain't no gunfighter, and I sure hope he's not in the mood to try again. I've got a herd to get back home and time's passing. Are you boys ready to go?"

"We can go whenever you're ready."

"I'll get some more supplies together and meet you right back here. I shouldn't be more'n fifteen or twenty minutes."

"We'll go get our horses and gear and come right back, Mr. Smithson. It won't take us twenty minutes."

Dan thanked the marshal again for stopping Brady and went back in the store. Coleman gave him a tin basin full of cold water to clean the cut over his eye. He helped Dan put a plaster on the wound so it would stop bleeding. Once his face was clean, Dan could see that the cut wasn't bad at all—nothing like he thought it would be from all the blood that ran down his face

He bought a large slab of bacon and several loaves of bread, plenty for four days. Then, thinking about how young the Slades were, and remembering how much he had been able to eat when he was about sixteen, he added some extra cans of beans and peaches and some sugar for their coffee. He asked Coleman to pack the food in two cloth bags so he could tie them to his horse. When his purchases were ready Dan stepped out on the porch to wait for the Slade brothers.

He looked up and down the narrow street, paying careful attention to the roof of the buildings across from the store. Neither Brady nor the man who had been sitting on the porch with him seemed to be anywhere around. Dan shrugged his shoulders as though throwing off bad thoughts.

I'll have trouble with that scumbag again, sure as death.

The Slade brothers rode up to the store just as Dan tied the bags of supplies behind his saddle. Both boys rode identically marked ponies, smoky gray with black spots. The horses were small, not quite fifteen hands, and almost delicate looking, but their heads were beautifully shaped. They looked strong and spirited.

Dan nodded his approval and climbed on his horse to lead off. After about an hour at a fast trot they approached the herd. The Slade brothers immediately proved their claim to being able to work cattle. Dan found he could manage the horses and leave the work of moving the herd to the two boys.

By the time they got the herd moving, the skin around the cut on Dan's forehead had swollen so much he couldn't see through that eye. His head pounded so badly he called a halt early that night and turned his horse into a small patch of trees.

Dismounting, he turned to untie his bedroll and throw it against the nearest tree. "If you fellas are hungry, there's the supplies. Help yourselves. Just remember they've got to last us three or maybe four days. I'm gonna make this pony comfortable and find a place to unroll my bed. I've got to get some sleep."

It took four full days for the three men to push the stock back onto the Triangle Eight. When the herd got close to the western fence Dan rode ahead and opened the gate. As they moved inside the boundary, the animals seemed to know they were on home ground and trotted out onto the range to graze.

Dan looked with satisfaction as the group of cattle spread out in the lush grass. "Come on down to the ranch house with me, boys. I'll get you the pay I promised, and we'll find you a good meal and a decent place to sleep tonight."

"That's kind of you, Mr. Smithson, but we need to get on back toward home tonight. Our sister Bella is alone back there and she'll be looking for us by early tomorrow."

"I want to talk to my brother Henry first, but I think we could use you fellas as regular hands if you're interested in a job. You've shown yourselves to be good workers and the Triangle Eight needs some more dependable riders."

"We're sure interested in finding regular work," Joe Slade spoke for both brothers. "Paul and me have been scrapping for enough to live on ever since our father died. That's been almost two years now. Our sister's even taking in washing to make some cash money.

"Bella's an educated woman, but even though they badly need a schoolteacher in the settlement, the school board won't have her because of us. Her ma wasn't Osage like ours was. Bella's as white as you are. Her ma was our pa's first wife. She came from out East someplace. But since we live in the house with her, folks seem to figure we'll contaminate her and all of their children if they let her teach school."

Paul spoke up then. "Mr. Smithson, what we've got to find is a place to work where Bella can come live with us. She wouldn't be safe in any town if folks got to know she was left by herself all the time."

"Give me some time to talk to my brother, boys. We might have a solution for you if your sister wouldn't mind living so far from a town."

"She wouldn't be minding that at all, I know that for sure. She was happiest living on Pa's old place, before the bank took it over and we had to rent that place in town."

As three men led the recovered horses into the ranch yard, Dan called out for his brother. Henry, their foreman, and Jas and Tom, Triangle Eight's only two riders, rushed out of the bunkhouse.

Henry sounded out of sorts. "It's about time you got back here, boy. We were about ready to get mounted up and come looking for you. Who's the company? And what the Sam Hill happened to your face?"

"Hi yourself, Hank. I'm glad to see you too." Dan dismounted and walked over to his brother, holding out his right hand. Henry pointedly ignored Dan's hand, keeping his hands on his hips.

"You knew good and well I'd be worried out of my mind. What took you so doggone long to get here? Did you find the stock? Have you been in a fight?"

"Slow down some Henry—for goodness sakes. Let me introduce these fellas first. This is Joe Slade and right there behind him is his brother Paul."

Henry stared at the Slade brothers without comment. Jack Burton and the other two men nodded a greeting.

Seeming to finally wake up and pay attention to Dan's words, Henry nodded and said, "How do, fellas." He didn't offer his hand to the Slade brothers, but turned back to Dan to ask, "Did you find the stock?"

Shaking his head at his brother's lack of manners, Dan said, "I found the stock, Henry, even the horses, as you can see right here in front of you if you care to look. Every one of the cows are grazing in the top pasture and look like they're happy to be back home where they belong. These two fellas helped me get them here, and I owe them some money and a decent meal."

Without saying a word in response, Henry turned and started toward the house, calling over his shoulder, "Jack, you and the boys take care of this string of horses. Dan, you and these fellas come on in the house. You can tell me all about what happened after you and these men get something to eat."

"Take good care of those two spotted ponies, boys," Dan said to Jack and the riders. "Leave them saddled and keep them in the front corral. These gents will be leaving here right after they get something to eat."

Tía Inez beamed when Dan entered the kitchen, but her expression changed to concern when she noticed the bandage over his eye. "What has happened? Have you been fighting?"

"It's all right, Tía Inez. It's just a little cut and a black eye. I'm fine."

Giving him a dubious look, she said, "I am happy that you are back home, Danny. Sit down at the table. I will have your food ready soon. Here is hot coffee and extra cups for your friends."

"How are you, Tía Inez? How are those youngsters doing? Did you have any trouble with them after I left?"

Filling plates as fast as her hands could move Inez laughed aloud. "That Anne Marie seemed determined to fight with me at first, but she is calm and happy now. I promised her you would tell her what happened to her papa when you get back."

"Huh. Thanks a lot," Dan said, dropping his head, "I'm afraid she's not going to like what I have to tell her. I think her pa's dead. I found a dead man that was carrying a letter in his pocket with her pa's name on it. He's buried in that new settlement they're calling Severy City—the one over near the old Willamette place.

"I figured at first the man was the children's pa because of the name on the letter and because I found the tracks of a horse that was in that thicket where those youngsters were hiding. The man had coal black hair just like those kids do, but somehow or other his face didn't look right to me. I can't hardly believe he could really be their pa."

Henry frowned at Dan, putting his coffee cup down. "What do you mean his face didn't look right?"

"Both of those kids are fine looking people. You're bound to have noticed that. What I mean is—the girl at least, has a real quality look about her. It's kinda hard to tell yet on the little one. That fella I found mighta been what some people call handsome, but he had a sort of brute look to his face. I'm having trouble thinking he might a been kin to those two youngsters."

The group concentrated on cleaning their plates and didn't speak for a while. Inez replenished the tray of sliced bread and the bowl of gravy two times.

When Paul Slade finished his second piece of steak and sopped the gravy from his plate with another slice of bread he said, "That was an especially fine meal, ma'am. I don't know when I ever ate better."

"Thank you, señor. You are kind."

Joe took a last swallow of coffee and said. "You know something, Dan, you could ask those youngsters to describe their pa. That would let you know if the man you found was the right fella or not."

Dan stopped eating and stared at him. "That's exactly what I'm planning to do, Joe. Right after we go out to the bunkhouse and talk some business."

Turning to Henry he said, "I'm particularly pleased with the work these boys did for me, and I want them to come to work here on the ranch. I'd like to have both of them work for us permanently, Hank. They've got a grown sister living

over in the settlement they need to look after, and they want
to bring her out here with them."

Henry gave Dan a blank look and stood up to leave the
table. "Maybe we better all go on outside if everybody's finished eating."

The Slade brothers stood up and followed Henry. Before
he closed the door Dan turned to Inez. "Tía Inez, I'll come
back in the house and talk to Anne Marie and her brother as
soon as we get done with this."

When Dan walked into the bunkhouse he was surprised to
see that Henry and Jack Burton sat beside the table looking
at each other without speaking. They seemed to be deliberately ignoring the two riders. Paul and Joe Slade stood together in the middle of the floor, looking puzzled.

"What's this about you wanting these two boys and their
sister to come to work here?" Henry turned to Dan, sounding
annoyed.

"I thought I spoke right plain, Henry. I want these boys to
come work for us on the ranch. It happens they've got a sister that lives with them. That settlement is no fit place for
any decent woman to live by herself, and they need to bring
her out here where she'll be safe when they're working."

"What would she do here?"

"I thought she could maybe help look after those two
youngsters some until we find out where they belong, but I
wasn't looking to hire her on as a hand."

"Dan, I'll agree that we need some more men, but I ain't
hiring no baby-sitter for those blasted kids. You can just forget that to start off with."

Jack Burton cleared his throat and turned to look at Henry.

"We could sure use the men, boss. It ain't no more than two weeks now before we've got to start on the roundup. If we hired these boys their sister could live in the old foreman's cabin out back. It's been empty since I moved over to Sally's place last summer, but it's still in good shape."

"I hadn't thought of that. The cabin is empty since you and Sally got married, but it sure ain't big enough for three people."

"For heaven's sake, Henry. What's the matter with you? Joe and Paul can live in the bunkhouse with the rest of the men. I'm sure that's what they'd prefer to do. Their sister'll have enough room living in that big cabin by her lonesome." Dan looked at Henry and shook his head. He sounded thoroughly disgusted.

Henry kept quiet for a minute or two, looking down at the table. He finally raised his head to look at Dan. "Okay, I'll hire these boys for the roundup if they're willing to work for regular wages. That way I'll be able to see how they work and think over hiring them on permanently."

Dan put one hand on Joe Slade's shoulder as he said, "That's great, Henry. Is that all right with you two?"

Joe spoke for both brothers. "We'd be obliged for the work, Mr. Smithson. We'd like to collect the money Dan here promised to pay us for the drive. We'll be back here ready to work two weeks from today."

"How much were you promised?"

"Two dollars a day each."

"Good Lord. That's foreman's wages."

"Henry," Dan interrupted. "That's what I promised them. Please just pay the men and shut up."

Chapter Four

As soon as the Slade brothers were out of hearing distance Dan turned to face Henry, his face flushed with anger. He put his hands on his hips and his voice rang out harshly. "Brother, you and me need to have a serious talk about whether or not I'm entitled to any say in the running of this place."

"What the devil do you mean by that?"

"I mean I do enough work around here to have my say about running the place. I want to hire those boys on permanently. I told you that, and you know we need them. Besides that, you need to understand that I don't expect to be treated like I'm interfering with your business in front of other people—not ever again. It's downright embarrassing."

Henry stood up, his face white with consternation. His voice registered his astonishment. "For heaven's sake, Danny, what in the world's wrong with you today? I only

57

wanted to think it over before I jumped up and hired two men I didn't even know. I never thought of embarrassing you. You know that."

"I guess I do know that," Dan said softly, "but you did embarrass me. You always manage to embarrass me. Then you want to wonder what's wrong with me. Let it go for now, Hank. I doubt if you'll ever change. Come on back in the house with me and let's see what we can find out about those two youngsters."

Dan left the bunkhouse and headed back to the house. When he entered the kitchen he said to Inez, "Will you call those children in here?"

"Si, señor, I will call them for you." Obviously insulted by his demanding tone of voice, Inez gave Dan an angry look as she left the room. He could hear her heels hit the floor as she walked down the hall.

Surprised at her reaction, he turned to Henry. "I wonder what her problem is?'

Henry smiled mysteriously and shook his head, but didn't answer. He poured himself another cup of coffee and took a chair at the table.

Inez came back into the kitchen holding Bryce in her arms, accompanied by a young woman. Dan stared with his mouth open. It was the girl—the same girl. She had the same straight black hair and huge dark eyes, but she wore a blue dress—a blue dress that fit her. Suddenly—magically—she wasn't a mean-mouthed little girl who looked like a boy at all, but a beautiful young woman.

Henry began to laugh aloud at Dan's expression.

Dan finally reached up to yank his hat off and walked over to take his chair at the table, frowning at Henry. "I don't see any good reason for you to keep on laughing like you're some kind of hyena."

"There's no need for you to grump at me either, little brother. That girl plain fooled you good and proper. You might as well own up to it. She fooled me at first, same as you. When I got a look at her after Inez got her cleaned up and dressed her like a girl oughta be dressed I was so surprised I almost swallowed my tongue."

"Will you two stop talking like this child isn't even in the room?"

"Oh my. Please excuse me, Tía Inez, and you too Anne Marie. I guess I did get a little carried away with the joke. But you have to admit that Dan's a good target." Henry sounded contrite, but he continued to grin.

Dan turned to Anne Marie. "You are a surprise, young lady. When I found you in that thicket I could of sworn you weren't over twelve or thirteen years old. Remember? At first I also thought you were a dirty-faced boy."

"I'm seventeen years old, Mr. Smithson, almost eighteen, and I must say I don't see anything at all funny about this."

"Sit down here at the table with us ma'am—please," Dan said, his face serious. "I've got some things to tell you."

Anne Marie didn't answer, but took a chair across the table from Dan. She sat stiffly, as though she felt awkward or afraid, and rested her hands in her lap. She held her head up and looked him straight in the eye.

Dan cleared his throat before he said, "I found a dead man when I followed those rustled cattle of ours. He had a letter in his pocket addressed to Raoul Gillis and signed by someone named Andre Devereaux. This fella had straight black hair cut kinda long and had a nasty-looking scar running alongside his nose. It went right about here." Dan used his index finger to draw a line down the left side of his face near his nose.

"That was Pa," Anne Marie said in flat, matter-of-fact sounding voice. Her expression didn't change.

Surprised again at the girl's lack of reaction, Dan frowned as he continued, "Well, I guess I better say I'm sorry, then. The man looked like he had been dead for more than a day when I found him. That's why he couldn't come back for you youngsters—er—you and your brother, I mean, like he promised he would.

"I gave the letter he had in his pocket to Marshal Jenks. He'll be coming out to the ranch in a few days. He said he'd bring it along with him when he came. He thinks we can use the letter to help us find your folks.

"Anne Marie, I saw a big bundle of papers in that basket of yours. Will you let us look through them? There might be some information in there that would help us find your people so we can get you back home where you belong."

Anne Marie looked from Dan to Henry, her expression wary. "I know what's in the papers. I read them all while Bryce and I were waiting in those bushes. I didn't need to read them anyway. I know how to find my real father."

"Hey now—you wait a minute, girl," Dan looked puzzled and a little angry. "First you sound like a little kid and an ignorant one at that, and now a few days later, you're almost a grown-up woman and you're speaking altogether different. What's going on with you?"

"If you'll let me talk, I'll explain."

"Go on and talk then. We're listening."

"My name is Anne Marie Devereaux. Bryce is not my

brother. He's the son of the man I called Pa. The man you found dead was Raoul Gillis, as you found out from the letter. He married a distant cousin of my family and was a close friend of my uncle, Andre Devereaux. Uncle Andre is the man who wrote the letter you found in Gillis' pocket.

"When I was thirteen my father sent me to school at Miss Laura Maple's School for Young Ladies in St. Louis. Gillis came to the school one day driving a closed carriage. His wife was with him. He presented the schoolmistress a letter from my father instructing her to release me into my uncle's care, and naming this Mr. Gillis as my uncle's messenger. The letter said that my father was deathly ill and I was needed at home.

"The schoolmistress believed what the letter said. They even let me see the letter. It certainly looked like it was written in my father's hand. Mrs. Maple agreed to release me into Gillis' care.

"When I climbed into the carriage I discovered that the man's wife was holding a young baby—the baby was Bryce. I'd never been close to a young baby before and I became fascinated with him. His mother, Mildred Gillis, let me hold the baby and play with him. I'm sure they planned it that way to keep me from noticing where we drove. Instead of taking me to my father's plantation, Gillis drove to a farm out west of town. I had no idea where we were. I hadn't paid any attention to where we were driving.

"When we arrived at the farm Gillis transferred my bags to a small covered wagon. He ordered me to leave the coach and climb in the back of the wagon. I became alarmed then, of course, and I argued with him, but he took my shoulder in one hand and shook me hard. He told me that if I didn't shut up and get in the wagon he'd take his belt to me.

"I confess that Gillis terrified me. I found out later that his wife feared him as well. She argued against his taking me, I heard her pleading with him while he transferred my things to the wagon. She never agreed with his taking me, and she did everything she could to protect me as long as she lived.

"I went ahead and got in the wagon. Mildred Gillis made me take off my dress and put on boy's clothes, much like the ones I wore when you found us. She cut my hair off—short—much shorter than it is now. We left the farm imme-diately and traveled for days, I really don't know how long. We only stopped at out-of-the-way places.

"They never allowed me out of the wagon when other people were around. Every time we stopped, Mildred Gillis stayed in the wagon with me. She told me later that Gillis told people we both had some mysterious illness that he feared might be contagious.

"We finally stopped traveling at a place in the flint hills. I later found out we were somewhere northeast of Wichita, near the Little Walnut River. We lived in an old soddy that looked like it had been sitting there empty for years. It was an awful place, especially when it rained. I tried to run away from there once, but Gillis caught me. He beat me so badly I never found the nerve to try it again.

"As I said before, Mildred Gillis protected me as much as she could, but early this year she came down with a severe illness. A few months ago she birthed another baby. The poor little thing was dead. Mildred died the same day. That's when Gillis moved us into Wichita and started dealing cards to make a living.

"One evening he came back to the rooming house early. He swore and fussed that he had been fired for no reason. He had barely gotten in the room when somebody pounded on the door. He went outside on the stoop to talk to the man. I couldn't hear what they were saying. He was out there for a long time, maybe thirty minutes, then the man rode off and Gillis rushed back in the house, obviously excited.

"The first thing he did was pack all those letters and things in that basket. He yelled at me to grab a change of clothes for me and Bryce and hustled us out of the house. He put us on the back of his horse and we rode out of town. He rode directly east, and we ended up in that covert where you found us. When he left us there he said he had to meet a man he knew from St. Louis and would finally be able to get rid of me.

"I read all the letters while we waited in the bushes. They were mostly from my Uncle Andre. In one letter my uncle explained to Gillis about my mother dying when I was born and my father sending me to that school because he felt I couldn't learn the things a woman should know at home.

"The most recent letter cursed Gillis. My uncle wrote that he had instructed Gillis to kidnap and 'get rid' of me. He accused Gillis of lying to him for four years by hiding the fact that I still lived. I surmised that Gillis had written to my uncle earlier threatening to take me to my father if he didn't send him more money."

"We'll find out more in a couple of days when the marshal gets here." Henry shook his head as though he was ashamed to look at Anne Marie.

"I don't know what to say to you, girl. There's some low-down people in this world. That's an awful story. It's almost more than a person can take in. Do you have any idea why your uncle would want to do this to you?"

"My father is much older than Uncle Andre. He had no children with his first wife and he was old when he married my mother. She was years younger than he was. I don't think he expected to have any children. When I was born and my mother died the same night, Father blamed me. I lived in the nursery until I was old enough for a governess.

"He kept me at home until I reached my twelfth birthday. That's when he started looking for a boarding school for me. I resisted going away to school as hard as I could, and it took him almost another year to find the school he wanted, but he was determined that I go to school to learn to be a lady.

"My Uncle Andre obviously saw my going to that school as his opportunity to get me out of the way. I'm my father's heir, of course, but before I was born my uncle expected to inherit Château d'Arc, our plantation near St. Louis and my father's other property. I always knew Uncle Andre didn't care for me, but it took me years to fully realize why."

Henry looked amazed. "Child, you're telling that me your uncle hired this Gillis person to kidnap and kill you so he could inherit your father's estate and then Gillis double-crossed him and kept you alive?"

"Yes, Mr. Smithson. That's what I'm telling you. That's exactly what happened."

"We should be sending a message to your father, Anne Marie," Dan said.

Henry stood up and got his hat from a peg beside the door. Holding the hat in his hand he walked to the door. He stopped with his hand on the knob and turned to say, "Let's leave notifying her father until Marshal Jenks gets here. I think it might be better for him to send the message than one of us. Come on out to the barn and help me with some chores, Dan."

Dan stood up, "I'll go on out and help him, Anne Marie. Thank you for talking to us." Anne Marie nodded without speaking and Dan turned to follow Henry out the door.

Henry walked all the way to the barn before he said anything. Opening the door to the tack room he turned to Dan. "Do you believe everything that girl said?"

Dan stammered with surprise, "Of course I do. If you take the letters and finding Gillis' body like I did, it all adds up. Yes, I believe her."

"I don't know—I just don't know. It seems far-fetched to me. I'd like to read those letters she claims to have and talk to the marshal before I make up my mind."

"What motive would the girl have to make up something like that?"

"I didn't mean I believe she made anything up, Dan. I only meant I'd like to see some more facts, wouldn't you?"

"I don't know about that, Henry. I think what she said rings true."

"You may be right. Let's go on back inside. I didn't really have any chores. I just wanted to talk to you out of her hearing."

Marshal Jenks rode into the ranch yard late Sunday afternoon. The whole family was in the kitchen getting ready to sit down to supper. Anne Marie stood at the worktable helping Inez prepare the meal. Dan was filling a pitcher from a bucket of fresh water. Bryce sat on the floor under the table banging some wooden spoons against a tin cook pot.

Henry spotted the marshal through the kitchen window. He opened the door to call out, "Get down and come on in the house. It's been a good fifteen years since you've been on the Triangle Eight, Marshal Jenks. How are you?"

"Well, son, I'm downright surprised and grateful to hear that you remember me. The last time I rode in here your pa and a couple of other ranchers rode with me to round up that bunch of yahoos from up to Topeka. Those fellas were stealing your cattle and horses and scaring everybody about half to death, and I came in here to help find them. They were the same ones that were accused of killing that rancher and his wife down in Independence."

"I remember you being here, sir. I also remember Dad telling me stories about riding in a posse with you several years before that."

"That's right—you're exactly right. Your pa did ride with me on a posse once. We chased that outlaw Ches Whitley and two other owlhoots down through this country. One of my deputies got shot and I asked your pa and that Pretlow fella that was his foreman to ride with us. We tracked them fellas until they lost themselves down in the Osage country.

"It's good of you to remember me. You couldn't have been more than ten years old, if you were that, and your brother here was still wearing a dress."

Dan felt a little flash of irritation at the marshal's reference to him wearing a dress. He looked to see if Anne Marie heard, but she seemed to be ignoring them. He stepped across the porch to meet Jenks with his hand out. "Come on in and join us for supper. Oh, Marshal—I'm sure you remember Mrs. Pretlow, and this is Anne Marie Devereaux. The noisemaker under the table there is Bryce Gillis."

Marshal Jenks gave Dan a strange look when he introduced Anne Marie and Bryce. He stared at Anne Marie for a
long minute then turned back to Dan. "How about us sitting
out on the porch for a while so I can have a smoke before we
eat, fellas?"

"Sure thing, that's a fine idea. Come on, Henry."

As soon as Henry closed the kitchen door, Marshal Jenks
turned to Dan and whispered, "I thought you told me it was
two youngsters you found, Smithson. That there girl sure
ain't no kid, she looks near-about full grown to me."

"I felt every bit as surprised as you when I found out,
Marshal. You could have bought me for two cents when I
got back here the other night. There she stood, wearing that
same blue dress. It almost knocked me off my pins.

"That's not the half of it either. It turns out she's not really
that Gillis fella's daughter. She told us she got kidnapped
away from her father over in St. Louis. It happened around
four years ago. Her uncle, the one that wrote that letter I
gave you, paid Gillis to steal her away from her boarding
school. She says the uncle gave Gillis orders to kill her, but
he kept her alive."

Marshal Jenks took off his hat and rubbed the top of his
head. "Do you fellas think her story's straight?"

"I do," Dan said. "If you put what she told us together
with that letter Devereaux wrote to Gillis you can't help but
believe her."

"Lord knows son, I've been marshaling for near twenty
years, but I still have trouble believing how evil some people
can get. How come Gillis kept the girl alive if he was supposed to kill her? Could she explain that?"

"The girl told us she thinks that at first it was Gillis' wife that wouldn't let him hurt her. Then sometime early this year Gillis' wife died in childbirth and he needed Anne Marie to take care of the boy."

"I wondered about what would happen to the two of them as I was riding out here. What will you do with the boy when the girl goes home to her father?"

"Wait a minute now, Marshal," Dan's voice rose. "Who said anything about sending the girl home to her father? It's the girl's own uncle that paid Gillis to steal her in the first place, remember? He ordered Gillis to kill her. What makes you think she'll be safe at her home? Don't you think her uncle will try again?"

"We've only got her say-so about all that." Jenks sounded skeptical.

"Nope, sorry," Henry interrupted, "but that just ain't so, Marshal. I had trouble believing her at first myself, but she's got a stack of letters that her uncle wrote to Gillis. If they're what she says they are, they'll back up her story."

Removing his pipe from between his teeth, Marshal Jenks turned to face Henry and said, "She's got letters you say?" His eyebrows rose in astonishment. "The uncle was fool enough to put some of this mess in writing?"

"Yes, he was, and Gillis apparently kept them all," Dan interrupted. "Remember I told you that the girl had a bunch of papers with her? A lot of them are letters from her uncle, that Andre Devereaux fella. The letters were all written to Gillis. The uncle apparently convinced himself he'd never get caught in his meanness to put such things in writing.

"You have to read the letters to believe the evil. That man got plumb brazen about what he wanted Gillis to do in some of them. He cautioned Gillis to destroy some of the letters, but Gillis kept them. They may explain why he got himself killed. If Devereaux found out Gillis was holding those letters, planning to blackmail him, he'd know they put him in real danger."

"Yeah, I guess it's sure possible this Devereaux killed Gillis to shut him up," Marshal Jenks said. "In fact, I think it's a pretty good possibility. After Doc Tate looked Gillis' body over he told me that the man had been shot with a small caliber pistol. I thought that was a little odd at the time. Not many westerners go around carrying small caliber weapons. The only men I've ever known to do it as a regular thing were professional gamblers. Do you really think Gillis tried to use the letters to blackmail the uncle and he killed him for it?"

Dan leaned forward. "That sounds like a reasonable bet to me. You know something else, Marshal? I thought at first that Gillis mighta been part of that bunch of crooks that tried to steal our stock. His horse's tracks ran right alongside the trail of those cows for a good while. But when I caught up with the rustlers that skinny kid that was with them, the one that looks about fifteen, claimed nobody else was riding with them—that they didn't even know Gillis.

"That bunch of fools were nothing but some ignorant old hill boys looking to make an easy stake. They were too stupid to make a job of stealing anything. They coulda gotten away with that little herd easy if they'd acted like they had a grain of sense. I really think they were telling me the truth.

"Even after the boy denied the man rode with them I was still seriously suspicious about it. I questioned them two or three times about the coincidence of them riding the same route as that dead man. The kid finally admitted they had spotted two men on the way. He said they were riding in the same direction they were taking the herd, only a little over to the southwest of them about two days before I caught up with them."

"Two men, huh," Henry said, standing up to pace back and forth along the porch. "Wait a minute here. We better think about this carefully—if that other man the fella saw is Anne Marie's uncle, he's eventually going to figure out where she got to."

"How could he do that?" Dan jerked his head up, his voice taking on a note of concern.

Jenks stepped off the porch to bend over and tap the dottle out of his pipe against a stone in the walkway. Straightening up, he pulled out a folding knife, opened it and began to scrape the bowl before he answered Dan.

"You took Gillis' body over to the settlement, didn't you, son? All that Devereaux fella would have to do is look around a little and ask a few questions. He'd find your direction sure as shooting, and he'd figure out right away that those kids are probably here with you. I think maybe I better read those papers you said that girl is holding. Then we need to make us some plans."

"Come on back in the house, Marshal. I'll talk to Anne Marie right after we eat supper. She hangs on to those papers like they'll save her life, but she's sensible. If we explain what we're thinking, she'll let you read them."

"I'd say she better be afraid. If they're what you think they are those letters just might be putting her life in danger."

After they finished supper, Henry and Marshal Jenks followed Dan down the hall to his bedroom. He tapped on the door and called out, "Anne Marie, open up. I need to talk to you."

After a short delay Anne Marie opened the door, keeping her left hand on the knob. She stood on the threshold and looked at Dan and the other men without speaking, a wary expression on her face.

"You met Marshal Jenks earlier," Dan said nodding toward the marshal. "Can we come in and talk to you?"

"Are you going to show him the letters?"

"I'd like to, please. We think reading them will help us find out the best way to keep you and Bryce safe."

"I thought you said Raoul Gillis was dead."

"I did, and he is. But it's possible, and I'm afraid it's likely, that your uncle killed him. That means he's somewhere in this area. It may be you aren't safe here. The marshal thinks it's a real possibility that your uncle'll find out where you are and come after you here."

She looked straight at Dan and said, "You won't let him hurt me." He felt foolishly pleased that her words weren't a question.

"Of course I won't let him hurt you—not if I can help it. I think you'll be safe here, but we need to learn as much as we can. We think the information in those letters will help us plan how to keep you safe in case he finds out where you are and tries to threaten you."

"Come on in and I'll get the papers. I put the letters in the order my uncle wrote them. The Bible and some of the papers mention Gillis' wife. I think she must have been my father's cousin too, and mine, of course. That may be the reason she protected me, I don't know. I'll show you why I think that."

The girl opened the closet door and took the wicker basket down from the shelf. Placing it on the bed, she unbelted the top and reached inside to remove a large packet of letters. Dan guessed the packet held more than two dozen sheets of the same paper as the letter he found on the dead man. Anne Marie placed the stack of letters on the bed and reached back in the basket to take out a big Bible.

"Here's what I wanted to show you," she said. "This is Mildred Gillis' family bible. Her grandfather had the same name as my father. He was Julian Devereaux, too."

"Strange sounding name to me, but it's sure right there in the Bible, ain't it?" Jenks said. "That may go a ways to explain why Gillis was willing to help your uncle. Maybe he believed he and his wife were entitled to some of your father's property in some kinda way."

"That's something I never thought of," Dan said. "It could explain a lot."

"I don't see where it makes any difference at all," Henry said, sounding irritated. "We've still got to figure out how to get this girl back to her father without anybody getting hurt."

"Calm down, Henry," Dan said. "We'll do that. Just give the marshal time to read what Devereaux wrote to Gillis."

"Will you let me read those letters, Miss?"

"Of course I will, Marshal—here they are." Anne Marie placed the packet of letters in the marshal's outstretched hands."

"Do you object if I look through these other papers while Marshal Jenks is reading the letters?" Dan asked.

"Oh—go ahead. I looked through them a little. They seem to be property deeds; one is for a place called Beverly and the other is for some sort of mill. I couldn't help but notice that a different person signed each deed. I must say I didn't really try to understand them. My uncle's letters were much more interesting."

Jenks stood in the light of the window and slowly read each of the letters as Dan sat on the bed studying the other papers. Anne Marie went over beside the other window and sat on the floor to play with Bryce. The boy completely ignored the men and continued to play with some blocks and other toys Inez had found stored in the attic. Henry sat on the bed and impatiently flipped through the big Bible.

When Marshal Jenks finished reading the letters he raised his head and came back to the bed and restored the bundle to the basket. "I don't know what to think," he said. "These letters are without a doubt from the girl's uncle, Andre Devereaux. The name's the same and I'll take an oath that they were written by the same hand as the letter we found on the dead man.

"They make it clear that Gillis was working for Devereaux, but none of these letters actually say for Gillis to kill you, Miss. If we try to take him to law on the strength of what's said in these letters and what we know about him, we could run into trouble proving he intended for Gillis to kill you."

"I heard Gillis say that Uncle Andre told him to 'get rid of' me and I heard Mildred Gillis arguing with him about it. She kept saying, 'Killing the child would be a mortal sin.' That man kept me with him for nearly four years, Marshal, isn't that enough?"

"That's a lot, Miss, I agree to that," the marshal shook his head, "but you have to remember that you're still underage. Most lawyers and judges I've run into don't pay much mind to what women folks have to say anyway. Not even when they're all grown up. I can't rightly guarantee a court would even let you testify, as far as that goes."

Dan watched the expression on Anne Marie's face change from anger to disgust to dismay before she blurted out, "Are you saying my uncle might get away with what he's done to me? That the law can't punish him?"

Jenks looked over at Dan as though he needed a lifeline. He stood up and walked over to the door before he turned around to answer Anne Marie. "We just can't let that happen, little girl. Me and these boys are going to figure out what needs to be done. Don't you be fretting yourself over it."

"Don't you be trying to treat me like I'm a silly child, Marshal Jenks," Anne Marie stood up. "I'm almost eighteen years old and I have a right to know what your plans are."

She looked older suddenly—serious and adult. Her lips clamped together, firming her soft mouth and chin. Her black eyes stared at Marshal Jenks, steady and serious. "I insist that you let me know what you intend to do about notifying my father.

"I also want to know what you are planning to do about Bryce. I'm not going to leave him anywhere. You must understand that. He's my responsibility. I've taken care of him since he was a baby and I won't leave him."

When Jenks and Henry left the room, Dan walked back to stand close to Anne Marie. It distressed him for her to be so upset by their visit. "It's all right, Anne Marie." He reached out to touch her shoulder with one hand. "Everything's going to be all right. I'll go talk with Henry and the marshal. When we get finished I'll come back in and tell you everything we decide to do. I promise."

She turned and stared up into Dan's eyes as though by

looking hard enough she could see the truth. Shaken by the way he felt when he was close to her, Dan pulled his eyes away and left the room. He hurried out to the bunkhouse to find Marshal Jenks and Henry standing by the stove, warming their hands and talking.

Henry turned when he saw Dan come in and said, "I think you should ride with the marshal back over to where you found Gillis' body and help track whoever it was that was riding with him. If you leave right away, you can be back here in no more than three or four days."

"There's three things you need to know, big brother," Dan's voice was icy. "One, I've been riding almost steady for more than a week. I'm plumb tired out and I intend to get a good night's sleep before I go anywhere else. Two, I really don't want to leave the ranch when I'm almost sure Anne Marie's uncle was the man riding with Gillis and that he murdered him. Number three—and I consider this the most important of number of all—you two seem to be assuming that your job is to decide what to do here without consulting me, and I'm afraid I have a serious problem with that."

Henry's face flushed a dark red. "Now you look here, Danny." Hands on his hips, he stepped closer to Dan. "I know you work hard and you're worried about that girl, but doing a man's job ain't the same as being a man. You're still only nineteen years old."

"You wait a minute yourself, Henry," Marshal Jenks said. "I don't want to get in the middle of a family row, but if Dan here can't be counted a man I don't rightly understand the word."

Henry turned away from Dan to yell at the marshal. "He's my brother and you're absolutely right about one thing—you shouldn't be sticking your nose in family business."

"Calm yourselves down you two, for Pete's sake," Dan said. "I'm sorry for what I said, Henry, I know you're just taking responsibility, like you always do. It's only that I expect to be involved in what we decide to do. You know I'm entitled to that.

"I've also got a responsibility to that girl. I just got through promising her I'd keep her informed about what we plan to do. Then I walked right out here and you two seemed to think you have everything all figured without even consulting me, much less letting Anne Marie in on what you're planning."

"You're right, Dan," Henry threw one arm around his brother's shoulder. "We should have waited for you. I apologize, okay? We'll make sure you're in on it when we do any more planning. Now, don't you think you should go with Jenks here to show him where you found Gillis' body?"

"Oh yes—you're right on the money with that idea, Henry, and I'll surely go with him, even if I am dead for sleep. I only wanted you to acknowledge that I'm not your baby brother anymore. I've earned my right to be included in this."

"I said we should have waited for you. What do you want, for goodness sakes—to run the whole blasted show?"

"Hank, why are you trying to pick a fight with me?"

"I'm not trying to pick a fight."

"It sure sounds like it."

"Look, I don't where you get such notions. I'm not trying to pick a fight with you, that's all there is to it. Are you going with Marshal Jenks or not?"

"I'm going."

"Good. I'll keep the drovers here in the bunkhouse until

you get back. We'll keep a watch around the clock and be ready to defend the house in case this Devereaux character figures out where the girl is and tries to come after her."

After going in the house to tell Anne Marie where he was going and why, Dan packed an extra shirt and filled both his canteens. He walked to the corral to saddle a tall, rangy sorrel that could eat up the miles and left his regular mount to rest. Jenks waited for him at the corral gate, holding the bridle of a Triangle Eight horse.

"Let's get moving, Marshal. I'd like to get this over with as soon as possible so I can get a couple of days' rest."

Leading their mounts, Dan and the marshal stopped at the cook shack and begged some meat and other supplies for the trail. On top of a bag of regular supplies, the cook gave them a cloth bag filled with biscuits left over from breakfast and a big bundle of jerky wrapped in greasy butcher's paper.

Chapter Five

Dan led the way out of the ranch yard and set the pace. The horse he rode moved at a smooth, fast walk. He was so long-legged it became necessary for the marshal to urge his horse to a trot occasionally to stay beside Dan.

They rode north and then west until after dark. Too tired to cook, they ate some jerky and bread and wrapped in their blankets to snatch a few hours sleep. They were up and back on to the trail at first light. At almost nightfall the second night they reached the grove of cottonwoods where Dan found Gillis' body.

Jenks urged his mount ahead of Dan's as they entered the grove. As soon as they were under the trees both men dismounted and led their horses. Walking slowly, they searched for fresh tracks, but found nothing to indicate that anyone had been there since Dan left with Gillis' body.

Once he made certain no one else was in the grove, Dan left Jenks to check for tracks and set up camp. Picking up an armful of dead wood, he started a small fire. Then he used his knife to cut a limb from an oak tree and used it as a broom to brush rocks and sticks off an area near the fire to spread his blankets.

After roaming around in the trees until it was too dark to hope to see any tracks, Jenks came back to the fire and sat down to eat the food Dan prepared. "I found the tracks of one horse going off to the west. It had a bar across one shoe."

"That sounds like the track of the horse Gillis rode when he left those kids over by the creek. I noticed that the horse that carried his body into Severy City wasn't the same one I'd been trailing. I remember that kid rustler said one of the horses he saw was a Grulla. It could be his track. The horse I found wandering around in this grove was a big, rangy blood-bay. His feet would have made two of the one that had that bar on its shoe.

"Do you think Devereaux switched horses with Gillis?"

"Well, it looks that way from what you're saying, son. I don't know why he woulda done it, but I reckon it must be what happened if you found the track of this horse at the same place you found those kids. Maybe the bay ran away from Devereaux for some reason.

"We'll likely find out tomorrow. The next place for any-body to light going in the direction those tracks are headed is Taylor's trading post back over by Elk River. I think we should head straight there. Old Lige Taylor'll tell us if he's seen anybody new around in the last few days."

"Let's bank the fire and get us some sleep, Marshal. I'm bone tired, and I'd like to get started again at first light."

Lige Taylor's trading post looked deserted from a dis-tance, but when Marshal Jenks and Dan approached the building they could see that the door stood wide open. They tied their horses to the rail out front and crossed the porch to go inside.

As they stepped in the door, Jenks called out, "Where are you hiding, Lige Taylor. I came to arrest you."

A gravelly voice answered from somewhere in the gloom behind the counter, "Don't you wish you could arrest me, you sorry, trumped-up fake of a lawman. Where in thunderation have you been hiding yourself, Jenks? I ain't seen you in so long I'd begun to hope you was dead."

"Sorry to disappoint you like that, old man. Me and Dan Smithson here need some information."

"I ain't no dratted newspaper. I done told you that over and over, Jenks. You're all the time wanting information. I don't hear much way out here, you know that."

"How about you stop being so cute, Lige, and let me introduce my young friend here. This tall fella is Dan Smithson from over to the Triangle Eight. You mighta known his pa. We're out here looking for somebody and the tracks led us in this direction."

A tall man stepped out of the dark area at the back of the store and held up a lit lantern. Taylor's face was hidden almost to his eyes by a curly black beard. The top of his head shone as bald as an egg. Dan could hardly believe the man's size. He guessed he weighed more than three hundred pounds. He looked to be near seven feet tall.

Taylor stepped closer and reached over the counter to shake hands with Jenks and nod to Dan. "I think I've heard tell of you, son. Ain't you the youngster that's won the turkey shoot at the Willamette place for the last two years?"

"I reckon I am, sir. I made me some lucky shots."

"The first year you won mighta been lucky shots, but not the second. I heard some fellas in here talking about how it was. They claimed you're a regular Indian in the woods, too."

"I've had me some good luck hunting, too."

"Lige, did a fella name of Devereaux come in here a few days ago?" Jenks interrupted.

"Theys been a stranger hanging around the store here most of the time for the last two weeks, Marshal, but he wasn't too free with information. He never did offer to give his name, so I didn't ask."

"Can you tell us anything about this stranger, Lige?" Jenks took his hat off and scratched his head as he continued, "I shore can't imagine why anybody would want to hang around here for two whole weeks."

"The fella came in the store here first thing and said he had to wait here to meet somebody. He asked to put his horse up in my barn. I charged him less than a real livery would. He rode a long-legged bay—a fine looking horse. That horse was kind of skittish though. I thought he acted like he was afraid of the man.

"The fella just hung around and waited; sat right there at the bar every night. He rode out for a few hours every day and then set out there on the porch other times. That's all he did until one day early last week, it might have been Tuesday—to be honest, I ain't never quite sure what day it is.

"He went missing for two days and I thought he'd left for good, but I was wrong. The last time I saw him he came in here and asked to have his horse checked by a blacksmith. He said the critter needed a special shoe for a split hoof. He wasn't riding the big bay. I told him to ride back kinda northeast to that new settlement. I'd heard a fella say they got somebody by name of Stewert that runs a livery over there. They claim he's a fair blacksmith.

"The fella come in and had himself a drink and bought some supplies. Then—it was the strangest thing, Jenks—he asked me if I'd heard talk about a couple of youngsters lost around here. I hadn't heard tell of such and I told him so."

Jenks scowled at Taylor. "He asked you about a couple of lost youngsters, did he? I can't hardly believe it."

"I thought that sounded kinda odd. In fact it sounded downright strange, if you ask me. What about those young-sters he asked about—are they really lost?"

"Your visitor sounds like the man we've been tracking. He's probably the uncle of one of those kids, the young girl. We think he's likely been trying to have her killed."

"Trying to kill a girl kid? What kind of dad-blasted skunk is he anyway? I wish I'd a known he was that low-down, I wouldn't be needing no lawman. I'd a poisoned his liquor when I had the chance."

"I'm pretty sure the man you're talking about is the girl's uncle," Jenks said. "This crazy mess is all about who's going to inherit some plantation over near St. Louis. At least that's what we're thinking."

"You're thinking? I've asked you this before, Jenks. What kind of lawman are you? Are you telling me you don't even know why this fella wants to kill a little girl or even if he wants to kill her?"

"Shut up, Lige. There's no need of you getting so riled up about it. The show's already left town as far as you're con-cerned. Calm down and pour me a drink. How about you, Dan, you want a swallow of something?"

"I'd like a glass of beer if Mr. Taylor has any."

"I've got it, son, I made it myself."

Raising one eyebrow at Marshal Jenks, Dan stepped up to the bar. The marshal ignored him, concentrating on sipping his whiskey. The cool beer went down smoothly. Dan drained the glass and sat it down on the bar. "You should bottle this, Mr. Taylor. It's a treat."

"Why, I thank you for that, son. It's a real improvement for somebody to show some manners around here."

Taylor refilled Jenks' glass with brown whiskey and asked, "Are you and this helper of yours going to stay over for the night?"

"No, no thank you, Lige. I'm obliged, but I guess we'll just push along. We've still got a lot of day left. Maybe we'll catch up with that Devereaux fella if we keep moving."

"Have you got all the supplies you need? My prices are probably better than you can get at that new settlement."

"I don't know about that. I'd be willing to bet I buy your thumb with every pound of coffee I ever bought in here."

"That's a lie and downright sorry thing for you to say, Jenks—especially in front of this young fella. I ain't never cheated anybody on weight, not even when doing business with an Osage."

"Oh, shut up and bag me up a pound of coffee and a couple of those big cans of tinned peaches."

"What else?"

"Not a blessed thing," Jenks said testily. "If you'll wrap these things up we'll get ourselves out of here while we still have some money left."

Anxious about what might be happening back home, Dan urged his horse to a long trot. Marshal Jenks managed to keep his mount right beside him. Thankfully, the settlement lay between them and the ranch, so every mile they rode took Dan closer to home.

He was worried about what Devereaux might be up to. He agreed with the marshal's view that if the man asked enough questions in Severy City he would soon find out the girl was staying on the Triangle Eight. Thoroughly tired, the men rode into the settlement right at sundown.

"Marshal, I don't know if there's a hotel or boardinghouse in this town. We may have to sleep in the livery barn."

"Won't be nothing new for me, son. I do all right in a town that's got a hotel, but women that run boardinghouses ain't too much on letting their rooms out to lawmen. They're too afraid there might be a shooting."

"I know a couple of fellas that live in this little burg. They might at least give us some supper."

"That'd be a help. A good home-cooked meal goes a long way to make up for sleeping in a livery or worse places."

"Look at this, will you? The store's still open. We can ask about Devereaux there. I need to ask somebody what house the Slades live in anyway."

Three men sat on wooden boxes around a table in the back of the huge store building. When Jenks and Dan walked in the group stopped talking and stared. A man wearing a long apron got up and rushed over to stand behind the counter.

He nodded to Dan and turned Jenks to say, "I'm Coleman, Marshal, how can I help you?"

"I'm Jenks, deputy U.S. Marshal for this district. We're trailing a fella by the name of Devereaux. He shoulda rode in here sometime late yesterday. He most likely asked for a blacksmith."

"There was a fella here. He didn't give out his name, though. I mind it was kinda late yesterday morning. He allowed that his horse needed shoeing. I sent him on over to the livery. The owner over there ain't a regular smith, but he can shoe a horse."

"Did the fella happen to say any more about what he was doing here?"

"He did, Marshal. He claimed he was searching for two lost children. He said a girl almost growed and a little boy no more than four years old was lost somewhere around here. I told him we hadn't heard a thing about no lost children. I even told him it would be easy to get up a search party, if he wanted help. He said no to that.

"Then he said he was looking for a black-headed fella riding a tall blood-bay horse. I remembered this man that's with you bringing that dead man in the other day. He had his body tied over a big blood-bay horse."

Coleman turned to Dan. "I couldn't remember your name son, sorry, so I sent the fella over to the preacher's house. I figured he'd surely remember who you were. That fella rode out of town sometime yesterday afternoon. I noticed he had a couple of other rannys with him when he left. That Ben Brady you had the set-to with the other day was one of them."

"Thanks for your help, Mr. Coleman," Jenks said, motioning to Dan to follow him as he turned to rush out of the store. "Go find your friends. We've got to ride, Dan. That man headed straight for your place, you can be sure of that."

"I'll fetch the Slade boys, Marshal. You go ahead on. We'll catch you up before you get to the ranch."

It was about an hour before dawn when the four men rode into the ranch yard. They were challenged by a strident yell from the bunkhouse as they pulled their lathered horses to a stop beside the well.

"Hold it right where you are, you men. We've got rifles on everyone of you. Who are you? What do you want?"

Dan turned to Jenks, shaking his head. "That's Henry bellowing."

He put his hands up to his mouth and yelled, "Hey, big brother—it's me and Marshal Jenks and the Slade boys. We promise not to hurt you. You can come on out."

"Boy, am I ever glad to see you." Henry pushed the door open and stomped out onto the porch. Jack Burton rushed out right behind him. He had a scarf tied around his neck and rigged to support his right arm. He carried his rifle in his left hand.

Dan's face went white and he jumped from his horse to run to Jack. "What happened to you? How'd you hurt your arm?" He turned to his brother, "Henry—are Tía Inez and Anne Marie all right?"

"Hold on, Dan. Take yourself a deep breath and calm down, for heaven's sake. We're perfectly all right and so are Inez and those children. We had ourselves a little visit from that Devereaux and some other fellas early this morning, but we drove them off. He had three men riding with him.

"He came in here alone at first and allowed he was looking for two lost children, talking so sweet and smooth, slick as you please. He spun us this heartbreaking tale about losing those beloved children to a mad kidnapper by name of Gillis. He claimed he'd been searching for his dear little niece for years, trying to rescue the poor girl for his dying brother."

"You're sounding downright sarcastic," Dan said.

"Huh. You don't have any idea how sarcastic I'm feeling. We listened to what the bounder had to say, but didn't let on that the children were here. When he finished his story I just said, 'Sorry, we can't help you.'

"He must have given his men some sort of signal right then, because all of a sudden those devils started firing on us. They were hunched down behind that little knoll over beside the corncrib.

"Jack got that nick on his arm before he could run back inside the bunkhouse. The shock of it knocked him tail over teakettle. While he was down, Devereaux jumped off his horse and broke for the house. He got close, but Tía Inez had that light rifle you used to use. When she saw him coming she laid down a field of fire that made that yahoo turn himself around and run back over to where his men were hiding.

"We found blood on the ground right over there by the walk, but Devereaux couldn't have been hurt very bad—not the way he hightailed it out of this yard. He probably had no more'n a scratch, something like the one on Jack's arm. His men quit shooting as soon as he joined them. When we heard you boys riding in we thought for sure you'd be him and his crew coming back to try again."

"As soon as it's clear daylight you can show me where you saw the sorry snake last and I'll try to track him," Marshal Jenks said as he dismounted, stretching wearily.

"Henry, me and these here boys are plumb tuckered. I can't hardly believe how your brother here manages to keep on going. I know he's got to be beat. To my knowledge he's had about one full night's sleep in the last week. We've got to get some rest."

Henry stepped down from the bunkhouse porch and motioned with his good hand for the men to follow him. "Come on to the house and get something to eat first, all of you. Jas and Tom here can take care of your horses and keep a look-out for Devereaux. Soon's the marshal gets some rest some of us can help him track the devil down. We've got to put an end to this everlasting mess as soon as we can."

Tía Inez and Anne Marie placed a tureen of beef stew and a platter piled high with hot biscuits on the table as the men entered the kitchen. Anne Marie had on a white dress Dan recognized as one his mother used to wear. She or Tía Inez had shortened the skirt and taken it in to fit her. Her shiny black hair was pulled back to frame her heart-shaped face.

She stopped beside the stove when the men entered the room and smiled at Dan. He could feel his face turning red. The skin on his cheeks fairly burned. He stood still and stared at her for a moment. Then catching himself, he nodded and ducked his head to stare at his plate as he took his usual chair at the table.

Finally remembering his manners, Dan lifted his head to reintroduce Joe and Paul Slade to Inez and Anne Marie. As soon as the men took seats around the table he turned to Jenks and asked, "Marshal, will you consider deputizing some of us so we can go with you to track down Devereaux?"

The marshal answered Dan without taking his eyes off the plate of biscuits in front of him. "I don't know about me dep-utizing anybody, son. I doubt if I remember the right words for a swearing in anyway. I shore do need some of you boys to go with me though. There ain't much chance of me getting that sucker by myself if he's got a bunch of men with him. I can give you all a badge to wear. That's all you actually need anyway. I always keep some extras in my saddlebag."

Dan put his spoon down and hurriedly swallowed a bite of stew. Looking around the table, he said, "We can't leave this place unguarded to go chasing after those men. Devereaux'll take a different approach when he comes back, and I'm sure certain he'll be back. The more I study on this the more I'm thinking I should go track him alone while the marshal and everybody else figures out the best way to defend this place."

"What makes you think you could do anything different than I could?" Marshal Jenks asked, irritation showing in his voice. "I'll allow you're tough as old boots and according to your brother here, you're the best tracker in these parts if you are a mite young, but you ain't no trained lawman."

"I didn't mean that, Marshal Jenks. I meant we need you here, to help plan a way to defend this place."

Henry pounded the table with his good hand. "Just hold on there a minute, you two. I've been thinking about this. I don't think anybody should leave here. I think we should all stay put right where we are for now. We know Devereaux's going to come back, there's no question about that. So there's no need of us chasing around the country looking for him.

"I know exactly what we need to do. First, we need to put a couple of rifles in that little patch of woods down the hill below the house. If we did that I bet we could trap those lowdown varmints in a cross fire next time they try to come at us."

"There's sure to be a lot of shooting if he does come back." Jenks looked over at Tía Inez and Anne Marie and lowered his voice. "Shouldn't we try to get these two women and the boy out of here?"

"They're safer here than they'll be anywhere else," Dan almost shouted. "Trying to get them anywhere else would surely put them in more danger, not less. We can arm Joe and Paul with rifles and post them in the thicket out back. You're right about that idea, Henry—and I'll volunteer to stay in the house.

"As soon as I get some rest I'll go down to the cellar and make a place for Tía Inez and Anne Marie to hide with the boy where they'll be safe. No matter how much shooting goes on up here they won't be in any danger of getting hit down there."

"You're right, Dan, I should have thought of that." Henry shook his head. "You go on and get yourself a few hours sleep—use my bed if you need to. Joe and Paul here and Marshal Jenks can take themselves a bed out in the bunk-house. There's plenty of empty bunks. Me and the other hands will keep a close watch for Devereaux. I'll call you about sundown if that's all right with the marshal."

"That's fine with me, Henry. I thought at first we ought to start right out after that bird, but we'll all be better for a few hours sleep. If you fellas have finished eating, let's go on outside and let Dan go to bed. I don't know about anybody else, but I'm about ready to fall over in my plate myself, I'm so tired out."

Tía Inez and Anne Marie moved Bryce's toys into the kitchen so they could watch him and cook at the same time. Dan took the opportunity to sleep in his own bed. Inez mixed up a big batch of loaf bread and set it on the back of the worktable to rise. Anne Marie helped the housekeeper chop vegetables to prepare another big pot of stew. Following Inez's instructions, she stoked up the fire under the stew and put a whole ham in the oven to bake.

"Finish peeling all of these potatoes and about a dozen

onions, Anne Marie. You can dream about that boy later. We must get this cooking done while we have the chance. We will be hiding in the cellar when that evil man comes back and the shooting starts again. If we must stay down there a long time we will need this food."

"I am not dreaming over Dan Smithson, Tía Inez. I wish you would stop saying things like that."

"Danny is a handsome young man and he is a perfect age for you, señorita. He will inherit half of this beautiful rancho when he becomes a man at twenty-one years. I have seen you look at him."

"Inez, please. Someone may come in and hear you—please stop saying things like that, you're embarrassing me."

"I will stop as you say, little one, but I know what I know."

Inez turned back to the stove and continued to stir the stew. When the ham finished cooking she filled the oven with loaves of bread. It was almost dark when everything finished cooking. The fat loaves of bread were loosely wrapped in white cloths and sitting on the worktable. Several pies cooled on a rack on the dining table. Inez and Anne Marie began arranging the food in baskets to make it easier to transport to the cellar.

"Open the pantry door for me, señorita, and lift up that piece of painted canvas you see in the middle of the floor. There, do you see the outline of the trapdoor? Put your fingers in that slot and lift the door up. You're strong enough."

"This is amazing." Anne Marie bent over and strained to pull on the heavy trapdoor. As she lifted, the door revealed an opening about two feet wide and three feet long. A ladder made of rough boards led down into the darkness.

"You're younger than I am, girl. Climb about half the way

down this ladder and I'll hand you the food. You can sit things on that big crate to your left."

"It's dark down there, Inez."

"Go and get the lamp from the table in the kitchen. Give it to me, I'll light it for you. There's a lantern down there somewhere. I'm not exactly sure where it is. You should look for it close to the foot of the ladder. There's a nail driven in the stretcher on the left side. The lantern should be hanging there. Go down with the lamp and find it."

Anne Marie disappeared for a moment, then held the lantern up for Inez to see.

"You found it? Good. Hand it up here to me. I'll clean the glass and make sure it's full of oil. A lantern will be much easier for us to handle than a lamp for going up and down that ladder."

Dan opened the kitchen door and walked in. "What in the world are you two doing?" He had taken the opportunity to bathe and shave. Dressed in a soft blue shirt and clean jeans, he looked handsome and rested. He stood with his hands on his hips, and stared with a puzzled expression at the pots and baskets of food arranged on the tables.

"I am making sure that we have food to eat if we must hide in the cellar. Do you remember when we had to hide there once before when your father was alive and the raiders came? Sit down at the table and I'll fix you a cup of coffee and some food. I have fresh loaf of bread and dried apple pie."

"I'll say I remember hiding down there. I was so scared then I couldn't eat. I recall Henry getting mad as fire when Dad wouldn't let him come up here and help fight."

"Your papa was only protecting his son. Your brother always thought he was grown up more than he really was."

"Henry still thinks he can fix anything and everything. He'd probably set out to rule the world if anybody only encouraged him a little."

"Now Danny, don't fuss about your brother. He loves you—you know that. He is bossy, but it is only his way of taking care of you."

"I know that, Inez. He gets a bit wearing after a while, though. He forgets that nineteen years old ain't exactly a baby. I'll be of age in two years and half-owner of the Triangle Eight. He can't expect to rule me forever."

"He knows that, and he has tried to give you more freedom these last years. You know that he has."

"Well, I'm about to get seriously tired of him. He's awful slow to change."

"You're not fooling me, Daniel Smithson. You're only talking for Anne Marie's benefit. You love your brother as much as he loves you, so stop talking so big."

"Aw, Tía Inez," Dan whispered and looked down at his plate.

Inez turned her back on Dan and started passing the containers of food down the trapdoor to Anne Marie's waiting hands. Dan watched her work for a moment, then jumped up to help move the two large baskets over to the pantry. Standing on the ladder, Anne Marie stared up at him without smiling.

"Dan, please go out and pump some more buckets of water," Inez called from the kitchen. "The pump is much exposed. We will not be able to go out to the well if those evil men start shooting at the house again. You can hand the full buckets down to Anne Marie and she will pour them in the washtub. It's clean."

Dan balanced on the ladder as he handed one bucket of water down to Anne Marie and turned to climb down with the other. When he reached the cellar floor he turned to grin at Anne Marie. She stood beside the ladder holding the lantern high. He caught her eye and she surprised him by smiling back.

Keeping his voice low he said, "I'll be finished here pretty soon. We could play some checkers to pass the time if you want."

"I'll be busy taking care of Bryce. He might be frightened. Inez said we'd move down here and stay until my uncle is killed or you men run him away from here."

"That boy'll likely go to sleep early if things stay quiet. We could play checkers or cards as long as we can have a light."

"I guess it would be fun, we'll see," she answered softly, dropping her head.

Henry came in the house at nightfall. He seemed to be excited about their plans to resist Devereaux and his men. "Marshal Jenks is out hunting Devereaux and his bunch and those Slade boys are down in that grove of trees below the house, keeping watch for those blasted sneaks.

"Me and our men are going to keep a watch from the bunkhouse windows. Those boys are pretty good shots, and they've got sharp eyes. I don't believe anybody can get near the house without one of us spotting them, but I want everybody to go on down to the basement, just in case. We agreed that Dan should take the first watch down there."

Dan came in behind Henry, carrying his rifle and a double-barrel shotgun. "Thanks for telling me that, Henry. I had already volunteered to stay in the basement." Shaking his head in exasperation at his brother's obtuseness he continued, "We're ready to hole up. Tía Inez is using my old rifle and I loaded up Dad's pistol and that old Sharps .50 he used to use for hunting game. They're already downstairs, and I've got plenty of shells. We've got enough fire power here to wipe out an army."

Henry nodded in approval. "The boys and me have got plenty of long guns and ammunition set out in the bunkhouse, too. If Devereaux does have the nerve to come back we'll get him this time."

Accepting a basket of food Tía Inez held out to him, Henry opened the back door. "Go on down in the cellar, Dan. It's the best place for you to be. We'll take care of this. You just keep Inez and those children where they'll be safe."

"Don't you worry yourself about us, big brother. When it gets full night I'll blow out the lantern so I can see outside. I'll keep watch through that little window at the far side of the house. That way I'll be covering your only blind spot."

"I hadn't even thought of that. We'll know what to do if we hear you shoot." Henry touched Dan on the shoulder as he went out. "You be careful."

Dan looked around the kitchen wondering if they had missed anything. Inez walked past him, carrying the big coffeepot by its bail. She entered the pantry and leaned over the opening to hand the pot down to Anne Marie. Then she came back into the kitchen to pick up the short rifle from the table. Turning to look at Dan, she nodded.

"I guess you're right, Tía Inez. It's time. You go on down and help Anne Marie get settled. I'll bring the boy."

Holding Bryce in one arm, Dan tossed the boy's wooden toys through the cellar opening, then climbed down the ladder to the cellar floor. He sat Bryce and the toys on a pile of blankets and stepped back up the ladder far enough to reach over his head and pull the trapdoor closed.

As he stepped off the ladder onto the cellar floor he heard Henry's footsteps. He walked across the kitchen and into the pantry. Dan grinned when he heard the thump of a barrel or something else heavy landing on the trapdoor.

Henry's making sure everything's covered. He's hidden that entrance to the cellar in case Devereaux or his men should get past him somehow.

Only one other entrance to the cellar existed. That entrance lay well hidden in the same patch of woods where the Slade brothers stood watch. Dan and Henry's grandfather dug the escape tunnel when he built the original cabin. That cabin now served as the ranch house kitchen and pantry, giving access to the cellar and the tunnel. Back then, Indian trouble came to outlying ranches regularly. Indians often set cabins on fire when well-armed settlers put up a tough fight. It was imperative to provide an escape route.

Earlier that afternoon Dan had unbarred the door to the tunnel to crawl through and make sure it was still passable. He didn't go out of the tunnel opening into the trees, but went far enough to look through the bushes that hid the opening, satisfying himself that the escape route was clear of large obstacles so they could crawl through if it became necessary. After he checked the tunnel, he closed the heavy door and barred it again.

He knew Devereaux was desperate. The man certainly realized that if he left Anne Marie alive she knew enough to send him to prison. It's possible he thought she knew enough to get him hanged. Dan was sure that Devereaux could have no idea Gillis left that packet of letters as evidence. He couldn't know that the law already had enough evidence to convict him for the kidnapping without Anne Marie's testimony.

Devereaux must believe that if he kills Anne Marie he'll be safe, that no one will be able to prove his involvement in what Gillis did to her. It must be that, or he wouldn't take the chance of attacking the ranch. Either that or he's really crazy. That may be it—he's driven himself crazy over this thing. I'll bet he'll be back for Anne Marie and won't care who he hurts trying to get her.

Chapter Six

Dan, Anne Marie, and Inez played card games until Inez complained of sleepiness. Bryce was already curled up on his blankets and snored softly. Anne Marie and Inez made themselves a pallet beside him and were soon asleep.

A little after midnight Dan began to feel so tired and weak he leaned back against the ladder and dozed. He kept shaking his head, even hit the heel of his hand against the side of his head, but no matter how hard he tried to stay awake his head kept drooping.

The air in the cellar smelled stale. He couldn't seem to get a full breath. Struggling to his feet, he paced the length of the cellar again and again, trying to clear his head.

I don't know what's the matter with me. Maybe if I stay on my feet I'll be able to stay awake—maybe I'll be able to breathe better.

Going back to his post beside the narrow window, Dan leaned against the logs. He could see a fair distance in the moonlight, but nothing moved. The opening was only about four inches high and two feet long—nothing but a gap in the foundation logs covered by a fixed piece of glass. It gave him a narrow but wide field of vision.

Suddenly breathless again, Dan felt a wild urge to drive his rifle barrel through the glass to let the cool night air fill the cellar. He couldn't get enough air.

Turning to the back of the cellar, he lifted the heavy oak beam out of the iron brackets on each side of the tunnel opening. Suddenly weak, he dropped the bar to one side so he could pull the door open. Cool air rushed in. He gratefully filled his lungs, taking deep breaths of the sweet fresh air over and over. After a moment or two he began to feel wide awake again.

Breathing in the air gave Dan a coughing fit. When he finally stopped hacking, he closed his eyes and leaned against the jamb of the tunnel door to rest, thankful to be able to breathe freely.

Suddenly, he could feel a presence nearby. Someone or something was in the tunnel. Before he could move something struck him in the side. A gruff and strained voice whispered in his ear, "Get your hands up, Smithson, and don't make a sound."

Dan felt a pistol barrel pressing hard against his ribs. Inez started to swing her rifle up, but the man grabbed Dan's shoulder with his left hand and pulled him around in front of him as a shield. He moved the pistol to hold the barrel against the back of Dan's neck. He grinned at Inez over Dan's shoulder. Without a word she let the barrel of her rifle drop to point at the floor.

"Tell the woman to get rid of the rifle, boy," he said. "Tell her—or I'll kill you. No one will hear a shot from down here with all that firing going on outside."

Bryce and Anne Marie sat up and stared. Bryce started shrieking.

The man holding the gun on Dan said, "Shut that kid up, right now." He sounded out of breath. "I mean it—shut him up or I'll do it for you. Turn that light up some, girl, and get over here beside me. Bring the lantern with you. You're coming with me."

It was Andre Devereaux. Dan trembled with anger and fear for Anne Marie. "You can't take her Devereaux. Leave the girl alone. You've hurt her enough."

Devereaux pushed against Dan with the end of the pistol barrel, gouging it cruelly into the side of his neck. "You shut up. That infernal girl's the only thing that stands between me and everything I've ever wanted. If she's dead when my brother passes I'll inherit Château d'Arc and the money to run it properly.

"The infernal little witch was supposed to be dead more than three years ago. My poor demented brother believes she's alive somewhere. I've spent years trying to convince him to give up, to let her go, but he refuses to believe she's dead. I intend to take her to St. Louis and show him her dead body. I'll make him believe it."

Inez moved suddenly. Without speaking Devereaux turned his pistol toward her and fired. She twisted away and fell backward, out of the glow of the lantern. Desperate to free himself, Dan reached up with both hands to grab the pistol barrel before Devereaux could turn it back on him.

Devereaux twisted and pulled, trying to break Dan's hold. When he realized he couldn't combat the strength of Dan's hands, he released his grip on the pistol with one hand and swiftly reached behind him and lifted another gun from the waistband of his trousers. Raising that pistol high, he slammed the barrel down against Dan's temple.

Dizzy and confused by the blow, Dan thought he heard another shot as he fell to his hands and knees. He wasn't knocked out completely, but everything was blurred for the next few seconds. He saw Devereaux run across the cellar, but he couldn't see Anne Marie.

Shaking his head to clear his vision, Dan struggled to his feet. Holding the side of his head, he staggered to the tunnel door. Devereaux had the lantern. He could see the light flickering as the man scrambled toward the tunnel exit.

He couldn't see Anne Marie or Inez in the darkness. He didn't know if Devereaux had taken the girl into the tunnel with him or if the shot he heard meant he'd killed her—anything could have happened. He wasn't even sure how much time had passed, how long he'd been so confused.

Dan turned away from the door to find a weapon—his right foot struck against the rifle Inez used. Bending to grab the gun with one hand, he darted through the tunnel door and began to run. The lantern light bobbed up and down, far down the tunnel ahead of him. It gave him a glimpse of Anne Marie—of Anne Marie running behind Devereaux. The man held her by her wrist and dragged her after him as he headed for the opening at the end of the tunnel.

He almost reached the opening. Dan bent low and ran as fast as he could. Pulling Anne Marie slowed Devereaux, so he gained on him quickly. He got so close that he almost touched Anne Marie as her uncle slowed to climb out of the tunnel mouth, turning back to pull her out with him.

When Dan reached the tunnel opening he didn't even try to climb out. He could barely make out Devereaux's shape as he ran down the bank toward the trees. He had thrown the lantern to the ground. The bright moonlight revealed that he was alone, that Anne Marie had gotten away from him.

Dan raised the rifle to fire one shot. The bullet hit Devereaux and rocked him. He dropped to his knees, but only for a second. He jumped erect almost instantly. He wasn't badly hurt. Dan shot again and missed, miscalculating the range shooting downhill. Pressing his hand to his left side, Devereaux darted into the thick trees and brush on the other side of the gully before Dan could get off another shot.

Paul Slade came running out of the darkness. "Is that you shooting, Dan? What's happening? Who were you shooting at?"

"Devereaux. He got in the house through the tunnel. I don't know what happened exactly. I've got to find out where Anne Marie got to."

"She's right here, Dan. She got away from the man when he started to climb out of the tunnel. She took off so fast she barreled right into me." When Paul came closer Dan could see him holding Anne Marie's hand. His brother was right behind him.

Dan hurried to Anne Marie. He grasped her shoulders with both hands. "Are you all right? How did you get away from him?" Overcome with relief, he suddenly felt almost too weak to stand.

Anne Marie pulled her hand from Slade's and leaned against Dan. He felt her whole body shaking as he wrapped his arms around her.

"It's all right now," he whispered, "you can stop trembling. Devereaux's gone."

She dropped her head against his chest. "He's still alive, isn't he?"

"I'm sorry to have to say it, but yes, he's still alive."

"When he grabbed me, I almost fainted I was so afraid. Oh, Dan, I was so afraid he would shoot you. I prayed you would kill him."

"Don't be so bloodthirsty, little one. Come on—we've got to hurry back inside and see about Tía Inez."

"Oh my goodness—yes—yes. I can't believe I forgot about her. Get the lantern, Dan. We must hurry."

Dan turned to the Slade brothers. "You boys stay down here for about an another hour then come on up to the bunkhouse. Keep your eyes open. I know I hit Devereaux, but I don't think I did any serious damage. He could still run, so it stands to reason he can still use a gun. I'm going back through the tunnel. I'll barricade the inside door."

Anne Marie ran easily through the tunnel. Dan's height forced him to stoop so low he moved awkwardly, but he managed to stay close behind her. When he reached the opening to the basement she had dropped to her knees beside Inez. Henry knelt at her other side. He held a screaming Bryce in his arms.

"Is she all right?" Dan asked.

"You can ask me. I'm awake." Inez sounded irritated.

"It sounds as if you're as mean as ever, so you must be all right."

"It's only a crease, Danny, I promise. It is nothing serious. I'll have a new part in my hair, right over the top of my right ear."

"Henry, I feel like a complete fool. The air got so bad down here I got to feeling like I couldn't breathe. I opened the tunnel door to get some fresh air. Devereaux was waiting right outside the door and jumped me before I could do anything. How in the world could he know about this tunnel?"

"Believe it or not, that's easy to explain. That youngest Johnston boy rode with Devereaux's men. Inez just told me the boy was with us the last time the raiders came and Ma and Pa hid us down here. Some more of the neighbors' kids were here with us too.

"Johnston was only a little shaver when it happened. It's a puzzle to me that he would remember the tunnel at all. He spent two days hiding down here with us that time. It must have made a big impression on him. You couldn't have been over two or three years old when it happened."

"That bunch of lowlifes always did hate us." Dan shook his head. "Do you suppose Devereaux told Johnston he was after killing this girl?"

"I doubt that, I really do. Even a Johnston would draw the line on hunting a youngster, especially a girl. Devereaux probably just told him he was after us. As much as they hate us, any one of them would have jumped at that."

"Did you capture Johnston?"

"Not exactly."

"What does that mean?"

"I killed him."

"Was anybody else hurt?"

"None of our men were touched, thank goodness," Henry said. "Devereaux set three men to attack the bunkhouse. I guess their plan was to give him cover while he came in through the tunnel. All three of those men are dead, I'm afraid. Marshal Jenks worked his way around behind them. Once he opened up with his rifle they had to move and the only place to go was right into our guns. They didn't have a bluebird's chance in Hades.

"Let's get Inez and the kids upstairs, Dan. I'll help you with Tía Inez. Don't worry about the food now, we'll get that back upstairs in the morning. If you hit Devereaux hard enough to knock him down I don't think we need to worry about him for a couple of days.

"Anne Marie, can you take Bryce up the ladder and get him to shut up his hollering?"

Dan helped Inez to her feet and steadied her with an arm around her shoulders. Henry went ahead of them up the ladder. Inez managed to crawl up slowly, rung by rung. Dan kept his hands on her shoulder and back to steady her until Henry could reach down from the pantry to take her hand and help her through the trapdoor.

Following Inez upstairs, Dan entered the pantry and closed the trapdoor behind him. He replaced the rug and slid the heavy flour barrel over on top of the opening. He didn't think anyone could get in through the stout door that closed off the tunnel. Not the way he had barred it. But he knew he would always feel nervous about it in the future. He decided he'd take care of that escape tunnel with a couple of sticks of dynamite as soon as he could.

If Johnston know about the tunnel, there're others around that know where that opening is. It might be time to cave that tunnel in or at least block off the outside entrance.

Anne Marie helped Dan and Henry treat the crease on the side of Inez's skull where Devereaux's bullet scraped her skin. When they finished fussing over her, they settled her in the bed in her room and tucked the exhausted Bryce in the bed beside her. Anne Marie took a pillow and blanket and lay down on the rug beside the bed.

Henry and Dan closed the door and returned to the kitchen.

"Henry, I told Joe and Paul to stay down in the grove for about another hour. It'll likely be getting light by then and we can go look for Devereaux."

"Don't you reckon Marshal Jenks is already doing that?" Henry sat down at the table. He rested his head on his arms. He spoke without looking up.

Dan left him sitting there. "Go on to bed, Henry. We've got to have some rest, too. I'm going to lie down."

Henry went to his room to sleep a few hours. As soon as he got up he set out to take Johnston's body home to his family. He wanted to explain what happened to their son face-to-face. Dan walked out of the kitchen door when his brother started to ride out of the ranch yard. He led a horse with Johnston's body strapped across the saddle.

"Hey, Hank, wait up a minute. I'll go over there with you."

Henry ignored Dan's yell and spurred his horse to a trot, pulling the extra horse along by a rope lead. Dan cursed every step of the way as he ran as fast as he could to the barn. He caught and saddled his horse in record time, then led him to the hitch rail in front of the bunkhouse.

Bounding up the steps, he threw the door open and yelled, "Marshal Jenks, I'm going to catch up with Henry. He shouldn't be going to the Johnston place by himself. If that boy's two brothers happen to be at home there's liable to be shooting."

"You be careful of yourself, boy. I'll take care of things here." Jenks climbed out of his bunk. Reaching for his trousers, he yanked them up over his long underwear and strapped on his guns before he sat down to put on his boots.

"Thanks, Marshal. I wouldn't want to leave the house unguarded until we catch that Devereaux varmint."

"Go on, son. Catch up with your brother."

Urging his horse to a canter Dan followed the track that led to the Johnston's holding. After a few minutes he caught sight of Henry. When he caught up he slowed his horse to a trot and rode alongside him.

Henry's face was flushed with anger when he turned to Dan. "Go on back home, Dan, for heaven's sake. Go on back home—right now. I'll take care of this."

"We'll take care of this, big brother," Dan said. "Those Johnstons are trigger happy on top of being sneaky. Burt and Williard Johnston might be a little slow on brainpower, but they're tough fighting men. That whole family's going to be hard hit when they find out Calvin's dead. He's their youngest. They'll be looking to pay somebody back for killing him."

"Bill and Martha Johnston are sensible people," Henry said. "They'll be broken up about losing their son—I know that, but they'll understand once I explain how it happened. It's plain we did the only thing we could."

"I think you're being downright silly."

"Don't you be calling me silly, Daniel Smithson."

"Well, shut up about it then. I'm going with you and that's all there is to it."

"You're certainly getting uppity lately."

"Oh, for goodness sake, Henry." Dan urged his horse ahead as he called over his shoulder, "Just shut the heck up."

The Johnston homestead lay in the shade of a grove of ancient pecan trees. Several long dead branches lay in the yard, close to the front porch. The house and outbuildings revealed the ravages of years of neglect. Twisted boards hung off one side of the barn. Two corral posts leaned dangerously close to the dirt and the gate was held shut with twisted wire.

The only animals in sight were two swaybacked mules standing hip-shot in muck up to their hocks and a rake thin black-and-white mongrel dog. The dog barked wildly and ran out of the barn with five pups nipping at her heels. She stopped at the corner of the house and dropped back on her haunches, snarling defiance.

When he stopped to open the sagging gate that led into the Johnston's yard, Henry turned to Dan and said, "Hang back a little, since you have to be here. We shouldn't be standing too close together in case you're right."

"Okay, you go ahead and hail the house, I'll stay right here."

Bill Johnston stepped out onto the porch in response to Henry's hello. A tall, heavy man, he had to duck to avoid hitting his head on the lintel as he came through the cabin door. He held a shotgun in one hand, its barrel pointed at the floor.

"Who you fellas got under the tarp on that there horse?" Johnston's voice boomed out, loud and angry sounding.

"I'm afraid it's your Calvin, Mr. Johnston. He rode with some men that tried to raid our place last night. They were trying to kill a young girl."

"You're a liar." Johnston's expression turned ugly.

"No, sir. I am not a liar. Your son took money from a fella to help him attack our place. You'll find the money in his shirt pocket. We shot to defend ourselves. We didn't know

Calvin was even in the fight until we found his body after the attack was over."

"You two stand down off your horses," Johnston said, starting to lift the shotgun, "this Greener's loaded with buckshot."

"We're not getting down under your gun, Mr. Johnston." Dan urged his horse closer to Henry's side. "You keep that shotgun pointed down at the floor just like it is now." He had his Colt out and leveled at Johnston's head.

Martha Johnston stepped out on the porch. Thin as a rail and almost as tall as her husband, she had obviously been listening, because her face contorted in anger. "Stop acting like a fool, Bill Johnston. Them two devils will kill us both out of hand if you don't behave yourself. Them Smithsons have been wanting to get rid of us ever since your grandpa settled this valley."

"We only came to bring your son's body home, ma'am." Henry said.

"Well leave it then, and git off our place. My other two boys will be home soon, and you Smithsons are gonna pay dear for killing Calvin."

"Yes ma'am," Henry said. "We'll leave, but you tell Burt and Williard this for me—we didn't have a choice about shooting Calvin—he was trying to kill us."

"You're dirty liars, both of you. Just like my man said you was. Calvin never rode with nobody but his own brothers, and he never woulda tried to kill no girl—not for no amount of money. When that boy left here day before yesterday he told me he was going to Ma Hainey's place to find Burt and Williard. They rode over there to play a game of cards with some friends of theirs and ain't been back home in almost a week."

Henry dismounted and moved to the side of the packhorse to untie Calvin Johnston's body and slide it gently to the ground. Still keeping his eye on Johnston, he climbed back on his horse.

Dan kept his Colt in his hand as they backed their horses away from the porch. When they reached the gate and turned to ride away, he holstered the pistol and looked over at Henry. "I'll swear my back is itching. I can almost feel that buckshot hitting me."

"It's your turn to shut up now. You're the one that insisted on coming with me."

"You're a blasted grouch, Henry. If you'd a been by yourself here you'd a had trouble with those two and you dog-gone well know it."

"I'm sure of one thing. We're going to have to deal with that skunk Calvin's brothers. When they get home and find that boy dead they'll probably come straight after us."

"You've got that right."

"We'll worry about that when we have to." Henry spurred his horse to a fast trot. "Let's hurry up."

"Yeah, I guess there's plenty work waiting for us at home," Dan called after him.

"Are you sure it's work you're interested in?" Henry called over his shoulder. "I saw you making eyes at that little girl."

"Little girl! She's seventeen years old. Mama married Dad when she wasn't but sixteen."

"I didn't know you were thinking about marriage."

"Now you shut up. I didn't say that at all and you know it." Dan lifted his reins and urged his horse to a gallop until he was far enough ahead of Henry so he couldn't hear his brother's teasing voice. He finally slowed his mount to a trot, but stayed well ahead of Henry all the way back to the Triangle Eight.

As Dan and Henry rode into the ranch yard Marshal Jenks led his horse out of the barn. "Glad to see you back all in one piece, boys. I wanted to say hi to you before I left. I'm going to take Jas here with me and try to track that Devereaux."

"You be careful out there, Marshal," Henry said. "That man is a pure devil."

"You can say that again. I'll take care. See you fellas in a few days."

Jenks and Jas rode in late in the afternoon of the fourth day, empty handed and worn out. Marshal Jenks claimed to have been asleep in his saddle for the last twenty miles. "We found Devereaux's trail easy. That boy Jas is a good tracker, Dan. He'd give you some competition in that department. We found proof that Dan did get a slug in Devereaux's back down there in the woods, but the wound must notta been too serious. I found where he bled on the ground some when he pulled himself up on his horse.

"He was smart enough to lead the other horses along with him for several miles before he turned them loose. We caught two of them and brought 'em back with us. They're out there in the paddock. Jas said that Nez Perce's horse, the black one that looks like somebody mighta thrown a white blanket across his hindquarters, is the horse Calvin Johnston rode the other night.

"Neither me or Jas here had any trouble telling the tracks of Devereaux's horse, but we lost him when we hit that bunch of creeks that feed that big swamp down near the border. You know where I mean don't you—over on the edge of the old Indian Territory? Nobody could stay on a trail in there, to my way of thinking."

"Come on in, Marshal, and rest yourself a few days. We've all been staying up nights, losing sleep and chasing around the country more'n enough this last couple of weeks. Let's leave worrying about Devereaux to another day." Henry walked with the marshal and Jas toward the bunkhouse.

"You both go on in and get yourselves cleaned up and comfortable," Henry turned to say when they got to the door. "I'll go over to the cook shack and have Jim Hurt fix up some coffee and a couple a plates of food. He'll bring 'em over here for you."

"That would suit me right down to the ground, Henry. We had enough to eat, such as it was, but no hot coffee. We didn't take time to boil any when we were on Devereaux's trail. I guess we got too tired to worry about it on the way back home."

Henry joined Dan as they walked toward the house. "I'd sure like to know where Calvin Johnston got him a horse like that black," Dan shook his head in wonder. "Those Nez Perce horses don't come cheap."

"He probably stole it."

"You're probably right about that, but I guess it's possible he won it in a card game over to Ma Hainey's."

"Yeah. That could be so, I guess," Henry said, "though I heard that those boys are much more interested in a couple of the girls Ma Hainey hired to dance on Friday and Saturday night than they are in playing card games."

"I wouldn't be surprised at that either," Dan said, chuckling. "Jas told me she had a couple of real lookers in the last bunch that came in. He raved about them so much I've been thinking about riding over there and looking them over myself."

"Oh, for Heaven's sakes." Henry sounded completely disgusted. He turned his face away from Dan and fell silent.

Dan chuckled at Henry's reaction to his teasing. "I'll get Marshal Jenks to take that horse over to those Johnston folks later on—maybe tomorrow. We don't want to have to be explaining why it's in our corral if whoever Calvin stole it from happens to come looking."

When they entered the kitchen Henry walked over to the stove and poured two cups of coffee. "Sit down here with me a minute or two, Dan. I've been thinking things over. It looks like I've got to take Anne Marie to St. Louis to her father. It seems to me like that's the only place she can be safe. We can't stay inside this house and guard that girl forever. We've got our work to do. And anyway, keeping her safe is her father's responsibility, not ours."

"If anybody takes Anne Marie Devereaux to St. Louis, Mr. Bossy Henry Smithson," Dan's voice was loud and harsh, "it's going to be me."

"What do you mean, boy? That's a trip for a grown man. You might think you're all grown up, but you still ain't of age yet," Henry answered him with the same harshness. "You've still got to do as I say."

"Henry, I don't give a hoot about being of age and I do not have to do what you say." Dan leaned toward his brother, resting one hand on the table. "When will you give in? When will you face up to the fact that I've been doing a man's work around here for years? You know it, if you'd only admit it.

"You need to wake up. Just get this through your head right now: I'm taking Anne Marie home and you might as

well shut up about it because that's the way it's going to be."
Dan continued to stare down at his brother as though he
dared him to say anything more.

Henry didn't answer for several long minutes. He held his
head down looking in his cup and sipped his coffee. He finally sat the cup down on the table with a thump and looked
up to meet his brother's eyes.

"Dan, I guess I better apologize to you. I know you've
worked as hard as any man, and a lot more than some I could
name. You're responsible too. You're perfectly capable of
taking Anne Marie home to her father. I shouldn't have said
what I did.

"Tía Inez has lectured me something fierce two or three
different times lately about how I should stop trying to treat
you like a kid, and I know she's right. I guess I'll have to
hurry up and figure out how to break the habit." Henry smiled
and shook his head. "Suppose I put it this way—will you go
along with me to take Anne Marie back to her father?"

Dan grinned down at Henry. "I'll be happy to let you tag
along with me when I take her home, big brother, if you're
really so anxious to go to St. Louis. But first, we'd better get
our arguments in agreement so we can convince that girl she
has to go home."

"What do you mean by that?"

"Exactly what I said," Dan said, taking a chair across the
table from Henry. "Anne Marie told Tía Inez that she
wanted to stay right here on the Triangle Eight forever. She
says it's because she has to look after the little boy, but I
think she's afraid of how things might be for her when she
gets back home.

"She's been sort of running free for the last couple of

years. As the only child of a wealthy man, and a girl at that, there'll be all kinds of rules she'll have to live up to when she gets back. Remember, her father sent her away to that school in the first place so she could learn to be a lady."

"Well she can just get over that, and in a hurry, too. There's no hope for it. She's got to go home. You're the one who can convince her, Dan. Make her understand that we'd be as guilty of kidnapping as Gillis was if we don't take her back to her father."

"Me? Why me, for goodness sake?"

"Because she'll listen to you. It's easy enough to see she hero worships you."

"I think you're nuts, Henry. She acts like she hates me most of the time."

"Huh. You're sure not very perceptive. Tía Inez and I'll talk to her too, but you go talk to her first. Explain about us getting in trouble with the law and all and let her know what we're planning to do. I think she'll want to please you."

Chapter Seven

It took Dan and Henry, with the help of Inez, three days of arguing to convince Anne Marie to agree that she had to go home to her father's house. Dan sat on the back steps with her when she finally agreed to go.

"I'll go home. I know I have to. But I'm taking Bryce with me. He's been my baby brother for as long as he can remember. No one could expect me to abandon him now. He almost thinks I'm his mother. I refuse to leave him behind. No one can ask me to."

"What do you think your father will say if you show up with that kid?"

"I don't know what he might say and I really don't care. I will not leave Bryce. He goes where I go. If my father doesn't want him I'll turn right around and come back here with you. Tía Inez said I could stay with her as long as I want."

"But you're not even eighteen yet, Anne Marie. Your father wouldn't let you leave again. I don't think he's going to let

116

you keep Bryce, either; people might try to make something out of it." Dan leaned forward to emphasize his concern. "For heaven's sake girl, that boy's the son of the man who stole you away from your father."

"My father and I were never close, so I have to admit I don't know him as well as I should. But if you think he won't be able to see the difference between a man like Gillis and an innocent child like little Bryce, I think maybe I should just stay here and forget all about going home. No matter what happens, I'm not going to be separated from Bryce."

Dan finally stood up and started pacing up and down. He raised his voice in frustration as he said, "I'm not going to argue with you any more, Anne Marie. You'll have to straighten out the question of Bryce with your father when we get to St. Louis. We'll get ready and leave here as soon as the roundup is over. Every one of us will be going except Tía Inez. The marshal knows the route and he can act as your chaperone."

"My chaperone?—please explain. What on earth are you talking about, now?"

"I'm talking about a beautiful young woman traveling around the country with a group of men. It's just not done, and you know it. Your father'll want somebody in authority to be responsible for you, and Marshal Jenks agreed to do it."

"Men are so silly."

"Yeah, you're right, I certainly have to agree with you there." Dan turned away to almost run toward the bunk-house, muttering aloud, "That girl would try the patience of a saint."

"What are you so sore about?" Joe Slade called out. He and Paul sat on the bench against the wall on the bunkhouse porch.

Dan walked over and sat down on the steps. "It's nothing I can't handle. What's going on with you two?"

"Henry said we should take y'alls' big wagon with the canvas cover and go fetch Bella and our things out here." As usual, Joe answered for both brothers.

"So why are you sitting here holding your hands and looking glum?"

"'Cause we set out to work for you, and yer brother can be a real pill."

Dan covered his grin with one hand. "What happened?"

Joe stood up to pace up and down the porch for a minute, clasping his hands behind his back. "Nothing happened really, and there's nothing for you to be laughing at either. It's only that I didn't forgot how to do everything because I agreed to come to work here, and yer brother seems to think I did."

"Come on, Joe, please let it pass. We need this job." Paul left the bench to stand beside Joe. They both faced Dan.

"It's all right, Paul," Dan said, working to keep a straight face, "I'll take care of this. Joe, remember this, you won't be called on to work closely with Henry. The last few days aren't the way we normally work."

Dan stood up and placed his right hand on Joe's shoulder. "You'll work directly for Jack Burton. He's the ranch foreman and I know from experience that he'll treat you right. Henry's just bossy. I reckon it's a problem he can't control. He and I fight about it all the time. I'll talk to him."

"I guess I'll stick with Paul. We do need this job—it's perfect for us because of that cabin for Bella to live in. I guess I kinda got scared thinking that if your brother really runs the place, he might be riding my back all the time, and I know I couldn't stand that for long, no matter how much I need the job."

"The Triangle Eight belongs to me and Henry together, even-steven. Henry really is a good man, Joe, even if he is aggravating. I'll swear, he doesn't have any idea how much he riles people with his bossiness.

"Tell you what, fellas. Come on. I'll help you get the wagon ready so you can go get your sister moved out here. Time you get to Severy City and get the wagon loaded it'll be late tomorrow night before you get back.

"I'll also make it up with Tía Inez for your sister to stay in the house that first night, and you can help me get her stuff unloaded and the cabin ready for her to move into the next day. Me and Henry and all of us can sleep in the bunkhouse for that one night."

Joe's expression cleared. "Bella wouldn't want to be no trouble to anybody."

"She won't be any trouble, Joe. Don't be silly," Dan said. "Tía Inez will love having another woman to talk to. She always complains that it's lonesome when we're out working. She's sure to be lonesome after Anne Marie and Bryce leave. She isn't going with us to St. Louis either, so your sister'll be company for her while we're gone. I'll feel a whole lot better for somebody like you boys and your sister to be here with her."

"When are you folks leaving for St. Louis?" Joe asked.

"As soon as we can finish with this roundup. We're actually making up a smaller herd than usual and sending Jack Burton on to Wichita to take care of selling the steers instead of going ourselves like we ordinarily would. That'll free us up so we can leave here sooner. Jack can manage fine with you boys helping him, that little scratch on his shoulder is almost healed. It ain't much more than a week's drive to Wichita at the worst, and Jack's been over the ground plenty of times.

"Me and Henry both plan to go with Anne Marie to St. Louis. Marshal Jenks agreed to get back to the ranch by the time we finish with the roundup. He's going to make the trip with us. He'll sort of speak for us to the law when we get down there. We don't know anybody in St. Louis and having the marshal with us might be help, especially if the law has trouble believing some of the crazy things that's happened. Jenks said he had to ride down to Coffeyville to take care of some business. He'll be leaving here at first light tomorrow."

Tía Inez and Anne Marie placed supper on the table just before they noticed the wagon carrying the Slades' belongings pulling into the ranch yard. Henry and Dan walked outside to watch. Paul Slade rode a little ahead of the wagon. Joe drove the team. A tall girl sat beside him on the high seat.

Henry stepped down from the back porch and walked closer to the wagon. He looked up at Bella Slade and stopped to stare. Dan gasped in astonishment when he noticed that Henry's entire body jerked when he looked at the woman as though he'd felt a shock.

Joe swung the horses around in a wide circle and parked the wagon at the far end of the bunkhouse, out of everyone's way. He jumped down from the high seat and turned to reach both arms up, placed his hands around his sister's waist, and swung her to the ground.

Bella Slade was as different from Joe and Paul as night is from day. The setting sun seemed to reflect on her long, pale hair, creating a golden glow around her face. When Henry walked close enough to touch her he stopped and continued to stare, still without speaking, never taking his eyes from her face.

When Dan reached Henry's side he caught his brother's arm and gave it a shake. "Stop this, Henry, for heaven's sake," he whispered. "Say hello or something before the woman thinks you're a complete idiot."

Henry shook his head as though to wake himself up and blurted out, "Hello Miz Slade, welcome to the Triangle Eight." His voice sounded like he needed to clear his throat.

Dan stood beside Henry, smiling a welcome. "Come on in the house Miz Slade—supper's almost ready. We thought you might get here about now, and Tía Inez and her helper put your name in the pot."

Bella Slade didn't even turn her head to look at Dan. Her blue eyes continued to stare up into Henry's brown ones. Her answer sounded distracted. "Thank you, Mr. Smithson—that's very kind of you."

Puzzled by the woman's reaction, Dan removed his hat. "Please forgive my manners, ma'am. I haven't even introduced us. I'm Dan Smithson and this is my brother Henry." Bella Slade didn't answer him immediately, but kept on staring at Henry. Dan looked from one to the other in astonishment.

That woman seems to be as dumbstruck as Henry is. It's easy to see why the sight of that golden hair and those gorgeous blue eyes would stop Henry in his tracks, but why in the world would she be looking at him the same way?

Joe Slade took his sister's arm. Dan noticed that he actually gave her a little shake. She seemed to collect her thoughts and pulled her eyes away from Henry to turn to Dan.

"Thank you, Dan, I'm happy to meet you—both of you." Smiling sweetly, she continued, "I could easily tell you and your brother apart by the description Joe gave me while we drove out here."

Henry hardly spoke during supper. He either looked down at his plate or across the table at Bella Slade the entire time. Bella answered questions from Inez, Anne Marie, and Dan but offered no information and asked no questions. She seemed to have no curiosity about them or about the place where she and her brothers would be living.

When they finished eating, Henry rose from the table and moved quickly to offer his arm to Bella. "I'll show you the cabin where you'll be living, Miss Slade," he spoke softly, looking into her eyes. "I sent some of the hands to clean the place up and repair a couple of things that needed it earlier today. There's a good lantern in the cabin so you can inspect the place. If you find you want things fixed different I'll be happy to help you make yourself comfortable." Never taking his eyes away from Bella's face, he bumped his shoulder against the doorjamb as he led her out onto the porch.

Jenks and Dan looked at each other without speaking. As soon as Henry and Bella were out of earshot, Inez laughed out loud. "That didn't take long. Did you notice your brother's face, Dan? I've never known him to do more than smile and say hello to a girl before now. I've often thought he might end up an old bachelor, he's always been so shy, but he certainly did not act shy with that one."

Dan waited until Paul and Joe followed the couple outside

to laugh and shake his head in amazement. Turning to Inez he asked, "What did you think of her?"

"Oh, I think she's a beauty and she has a beautiful speaking voice."

"I think she's really attractive, too, with that mass of yellow hair and those eyes, but she can't be very bright. Why, she looked every bit as smitten as Henry did. She must have lived a protected life up to now, that's all I can say. I figure she's all of twenty years old at least. Surely she's seen better looking men in her life than our Henry."

"Now, Daniel, you be fair. Your brother's a fine looking man."

"You stop rolling your eyes at Inez, Dan Smithson," Anne Marie said. "You're not always the prettiest flower in the bouquet, you know." She stopped stacking dirty plates to look across the table at Dan, her eyes laughing.

"Well, thank you very much, Miss Nosy Parker. I didn't know you'd been noticing my good looks. Maybe you'll go with me for a walk down by the creek after so you can tell me all about it."

"Please don't get yourself too excited. I didn't mean I noticed you, or that I thought you had any good looks at all. I certainly haven't noticed you the way Bella Slade noticed your brother Henry. You can be sure of that."

Anne Marie seemed to stiffen as she answered Dan. She held her head high. The laughter left her voice and the tone changed, adding a sharp edge to her words. As soon as she finished speaking she turned to carry a stack of dirty plates across the kitchen to noisily immerse them in the dishpan with both hands.

Dan looked over to Inez. "What did I say?"

"If you don't know, you will have to figure this one out for yourself, niño." Inez rose from her chair and began to gather dirty eating utensils and glasses from the table. She kept her head turned away so Dan couldn't catch her eye.

Dan looked at both women in disgust for a moment. Then he rose from the table, pushing his chair back roughly. He slapped his hat on his head and deliberately slammed the screen door as he left the house.

Dan and Henry rose at dawn the next day and joined Jake Burton and the rest of the hands in preparing to round up the cattle they would send to market. They set up a special area near the barn to do the work and rode miles each day, collecting a herd. Before they stopped work each evening they drove the day's gather into a holding pen within sight of the ranch headquarters.

Carefully selecting only older steers to sell, they left the ones they branded in the last year's roundup to grow another year. Branding all the young stock they found, they turned them loose to return to their mothers.

The day Bella Slade moved into the foreman's cabin Henry began to disappear every evening. No matter how hard they worked on the roundup each day, he cleaned himself up before supper and as soon as he finished eating he grabbed his hat and rushed out of the house. He didn't return until everyone else had gone to asleep. Dan braced him late one afternoon as they were hazing that days' gather of cattle toward the holding pen.

"How in the world do you keep going, Hank? You've been up with the owls every night for over a week. I swore I'd stay up last night long enough to see what time you came back to the house, but I couldn't keep my eyes open that long."

"It's probably because you're sleeping in Dad's bed. It's so soft you can't help falling right off to sleep. Besides, I don't need as much sleep as you do."

"Huh. That's real funny," Dan said, a sarcastic tone to his voice. "I noticed you dozing in the saddle when we were driving the steers to the holding pen about this time yesterday. You've done it other days, too. It's a good thing we've got Paul and Joe to help us make the roundup this year. You're sure falling down on the job."

"I'm doing my part," Henry said, with an angry edge to his voice, "you just mind your own business. I've seen you walking out with that Devereaux girl almost every night yourself. You don't have any room to be needling me. If you're not walking around the place with her you're out back shooting or you're sitting in the kitchen reading or playing games with her."

Dan let the comment about his walking out and reading with Anne Marie pass. "I don't mean to be needling you, Henry. But I can't help but notice you've gone a little funny over that Slade woman."

Henry straightened up in the saddle and pulled his horse to a stop. His face reddened and he turned to face Dan to yell, "Her name is Bella and you well know it. What do you mean by referring to her like that?"

"Calm down, calm down now," Dan shook his head and stopped to meet Henry's eyes. "I didn't mean a thing by what I said and you well know it. Listen at you Henry, what in the world is the matter with you?"

"Nothing's the matter with me. I asked Bella to be my wife and she consented." Henry continued to stare at Dan, his face still red and his expression defiant. He looked as if he expected Dan to offer some objection to his choice.

"I reckon I saw it coming—we all did—and I'm delighted for you." Dan held out his hand to Henry. "I haven't had much chance to get to know Bella, but I like and admire Paul and Joe. I'm sure she's a fine person. I'm happy for you, Henry."

Relaxing, Henry grinned and grabbed Dan's hand in his. "I'm sorry to be so testy Dan. I shoulda known you'd say that."

"When do you plan to hold the happy event?

"Soon after we get back from St. Louis. Bella want's to make a special dress, and then we'll have to find out what Sunday that saddlebag preacher comes to Severy City and arrange to get him out here."

"Have you told Tía Inez or Joe and Paul about this?"

"Not yet. To tell the truth, I've been sort of dreading telling Joe and Paul. Bella says I'm being silly, but I'm not sure those brothers of Bella's like me a whole lot."

"Aren't you pleased with the way those boys are working?"

"Well, sure I'm pleased. They're hard workers and they're good with the stock. That Joe is a marvel with a horse."

"Have you told them you feel that way?"

"Told them?" Henry looked amazed. "Why would I tell them that?"

"You're hopeless, Henry—just plain hopeless. Go tell Joe and Paul you like their work—please? Let them know you think they're good at their jobs. Then tell them you and Bella are going to get married."

"What are you trying to tell me?"

"Joe and Paul think you're a little bit bossy," Dan said, breaking into a big grin, "and I can see exactly why they think that way. You talked to those boys like they didn't know the first thing about ranching when they first came here to work, and you sort of riled them, Joe especially. They actually thought about giving up the idea of riding for us because of the impression you made on them. I'm not kidding, Henry. Joe and Paul need to hear you say you're pleased with their work."

"Oh, bless Pete. What is wrong with people? I'll talk to them before we leave for St. Louis."

Dan and Henry stood on the bunkhouse porch and waved good-bye to Jack Burton and the rest of the crew. Jas and Tom started moving the cattle west at dawn. Joe and Paul Slade opened the corral gate and hurrahed a group of about a dozen horses along the track. Even on a short drive each rider needed at least two extra mounts. Henry had charged the Slade brothers with choosing and caring for the horses for the drive.

Dan had overheard his brother talking to Joe and Paul two days earlier. It made him chuckle when he remembered how Henry figured out a way to get around directly telling the two men he liked their work. He just gave them a truly important job.

He heard Henry tell them, "There'll be five men on the drive, so you men go through the horses and select at least three mounts for each man. Put them in the small corral so they'll be ready. Just use your own judgment boys, but make sure they're well-trained mounts, so you won't have any trouble keeping them together on the trail. Taking care of the horse herd will be your main responsibility on the drive."

It was plain to see that the Slade brothers were satisfied. Henry had done better than tell Paul and Joe he was pleased with their work, he showed confidence in them and in their abilities. Tending the horses on a trail drive was an important job in itself, but selecting the mounts for the whole group was usually the foreman's responsibility.

Chuckling again at the maneuver Henry used to avoid telling the Slade brothers directly that he liked their work, Dan moved up beside Henry and slapped his shoulder. He laughed out loud when Henry turned to scowl at him.

"I'm going in the house to talk to Anne Marie. I promised her I'd keep her informed of our plans."

"Well, as long as she understands we're not going to change anything we've planned to suit her."

"I'm not trying to change anything, Henry. Take it easy, will you? I'm just going to explain to the girl when we're planning to leave, where we're going and a little about what she might expect to happen on the trip."

"I don't see any need for that. She'll just have to go along with whatever we do anyway."

Dan turned and left the porch calling over his shoulder, "Shut up, will you, Henry?"

"You get back here, Dan Smithson. You promised to help me pull that new canvas over the small wagon. You're the cause of all this work and you have to help."

Dan ignored Henry and hurried along the walk to enter the kitchen. Inez stood in front of the stove, stirring a large pot.

"Whatever that is you're cooking smells delicious, Tía Inez."

"I'm making a feast to celebrate the end of the roundup—

the same meal I usually make when you get back from the drive."

"Hey, that's great. I'm about to starve anyway and everything smells wonderful. Where's Anne Marie?"

"She is in her bedroom getting Bryce to lie down for his nap. She'll be back in here right away. She is trying to complete some sewing.

"Sit down at the table, Danny," Inez said, "I'll pour you a cup of coffee. There're still a couple of those cinnamon rolls left that I made the other day. Do you want them with your coffee?"

"You bet I do. They'd taste good."

Anne Marie entered the kitchen as Dan stirred sugar into his second cup of coffee. Her expression was somber until she saw Dan, then her eyes brightened and she smiled. "Hello—it's early for you to be back in the house, isn't it? Is the roundup over?"

"Yep—all done. The rest of the crew left with the horses a few minutes ago. Everything about the roundup is done. I want to talk to you about our trip to St. Louis."

"Thank you. I really appreciate it, Dan. I saw you and your brother earlier working on that little wagon. I don't really need a wagon."

"Actually, you do need the wagon. We'll be on the road for at least two nights before we get to Neodesha. You'll need a place to have a little privacy. We'll also need the wagon to haul supplies for our meals and some grain for the horses."

"But I'd much rather ride. I'm a good rider."

"I know you are. You'll get plenty of chances to ride. Me

and Henry and Marshal Jenks will be taking turns driving the wagon, so you'll be able to ride my horse when I'm driving."

"Why can't you bring an extra horse for me?"

"I hadn't thought of it," Dan ran his hands through his hair, "but I don't see why we couldn't. I'll take care of it. Henry's in an awful mood. He'll probably throw a fit if I ask him. I'm not sure what's eating him; it's like he's threatened by anything I want to do that he didn't think up first."

"I know, I've noticed it too. Let me go talk to him," Anne Marie said, smiling. "I'll make him think he always wanted me to have my own horse on the trip."

"You probably can, at that," Dan laughed as he replied. "Look, I've got a map here. I want to show you the general route we'll be taking and explain in advance some of the things we'll be doing."

Spreading the map on the table, Dan indicated the route with his finger. "We'll drive east and south to Neodesha. There's a railroad there. We may have to wait a day or two, but we'll take the first train we can that goes east to Springfield, Missouri.

"I'm not sure how long it'll take us to get to Neodesha. We'll go over some roads that are pretty decent and some that will be no more than pig-paths, I reckon. You know how wet southeast Kansas can be this time of year. We haven't had too much rain right around here, but there've been downpours north and east of us during the last couple of weeks, so some creeks and rivers may be out of their banks.

"I expect some of the roads we'll take will be nothing more than rivers of mud. The wagon will be a problem at times, but we have to take it, all the same. You and the boy will be able to stay under cover in bad weather and it will give you a place to sleep up off the ground. We'll leave it at the livery with the horses when we catch the train.

"Marshal Jenks is gonna take the first turn driving the wagon, and Henry and me'll ride alongside. We've been thinking that it's a possibility your uncle will try to get at you somewhere along the way, so we'll be keeping a close watch day and night. That's another reason I want the wagon. If he should start shooting, it'll give you a place to be safe."

"I'm not exactly sure how I feel about this trip," Anne Marie said. "I want to go. I want to see my father, whether he wants me or not. But I hate to leave here. I love Tía Inez, and Bryce is happy here. He's not afraid here, and he's even begun to talk a little again." Dropping her head, she looked down at the table and whispered, "I'll miss you, too."

Dan reached over to catch one of her small hands in his. "We'll write. I promise. I'll miss you too, but you know you have to go home."

"I know." Anne Marie turned her head away, and wiped a tear from her cheek with her left hand.

"It's going to be all right, honey," Dan said. "I promise I'll write. It'll be less than two years until I'm twenty-one. I'll come for you then—if you still want me."

Lifting her head, Anne Marie said, "If I still want you— what a thing for you to say."

"Your life in St. Louis will be radically different." Dan looked a little sad as he whispered, "You're a beautiful girl, and your daddy's rich. You'll likely find some city fella you like a lot better than me before two years pass by."

"I promised I wouldn't, Dan."

Henry came in the kitchen door. He scowled when he saw

Dan sitting close beside Anne Marie and holding one of her hands in both of his.

"Is everything ready for us to start out tomorrow morning?" His unease made his voice harsh. "Isn't there something you should be doing to help get ready, Dan?"

Anne Marie stood up. "Bryce and I are ready, Henry, and Tía Inez has packed a food basket so we won't have to cook."

"Well, you better go ahead and get Dan to help you pile your things in the wagon before supper," Henry's voice softened. "We'll be leaving at first light tomorrow."

Chapter Eight

The sky was gray and the clouds looked almost menacing when Marshal Jenks turned the wagon southeast. Their route would follow a fence line that joined the county road at Ma Hainey's place on the first leg of their journey. Then they would follow the road east and eventually south beside Fall River to the little town of Neodesha where the Fall River met the Verdigris. Barring mishaps, their first camp would be on the southwest bank of Fall River, less than twenty miles ahead.

Dan and Henry moved out in front of the wagon and Anne Marie followed. She rode a dun mare that was one of Henry's favorite mounts. Dan shook his head in wonder—the girl had accomplished what she planned—she helped Henry decide that he wanted her to ride. Since Marshal Jenks had elected to take the first turn driving the wagon, his horse followed the wagon, its reins tied to a long lead.

The road was fairly dry and firm out in the open stretches

where the wind could hit it, and they made good time for the first few hours. As soon as the sun came out and warmed their shoulders, they all removed their jackets and tied them behind their saddles. Shortly after eleven o'clock Jenks turned the wagon onto the public road and left Triangle Eight range. Before noon, they were in sight of the saloon.

Ma Hainey's place was a big two-story cabin with a wide porch across the front that had so many one-story additions it looked hemmed in by little buildings. It was a combination saloon, eating place, gambling den and bawdyhouse. The hitch rail out front was on the edge of the public road. Five horses rested hip-shot at the rail. The black horse with white hindquarters that once belonged to Calvin Johnston was one of them.

The men would normally stop for a breather and to water the horses, but it was still early in the day and neither one wanted to risk a run-in with the Johnston brothers, plus it was no fit place for Anne Marie, so they agreed without speaking to keep moving.

Dan looked over at Henry and said, "That black and white horse standing there means at least one of the Johnston brothers is inside. I'm wondering about their timing. They may be looking to give us some trouble."

"I expect you may be right about that. Those boys proba-bly heard talk over at the settlement about us buying extra supplies for this trip. We'll still try to make Fall River before nightfall. There's a good camping place there that's up be-hind some rocks. It's right where the road turns to run along-side the river, and a place we can defend if it turns out we have to. I expect we'd better keep a sharp watch the rest of the way there, though."

"If both Burt and Williard Johnston are in there and the fellas that belong to those other three horses are riding with them," Dan said, "we could be in for a real problem."

"I kinda expected it," Henry said, "didn't you?"

"Not from them I didn't." Dan shook his head. "I surely expected trouble from Devereaux, though."

"You might be right about that, I guess. He could be sitting in there with the Johnstons planning to jump us. Let's go ahead and stop for a while as soon as we get out of sight of that place." Henry looked worried. "I think we need to talk to Marshal Jenks about this. Besides, there's some mighty delicious looking fried chicken in that basket Anne Marie put in the wagon, and I'm getting hungry. We really oughta take it slow the first day, anyway."

"Oh, I don't know about that," Dan said. "The travel won't bother us any, and Anne Marie and Bryce have got themselves a fine bed fixed up in the wagon. Maybe we don't have to worry about Devereaux still being in the area. I don't expect we'll run into him until we get well down the road—maybe even all the way to St. Louis.

"I guess you're right about the Johnston brothers. They'll probably come after us because of their brother. If they knew we'd be headed this way after we finished the roundup they coulda decided hole up over here and watch out for us."

"Maybe you're right, Dan—I just don't know. But those boys hang around over here about half their time anyway. They could be just gambling and visiting Ma's girls like they usually do. I agree we should talk to Jenks though. Why don't you go ahead and drop back behind the wagon with that girl and kinda keep a watch on our back trail."

Dan guided his horse to the rear of the wagon and rode

beside Anne Marie until Henry waved to Marshal Jenks to turn the wagon and park it close up under a patch of cotton-wood trees. "There's some sweet water in a little spring here," Henry said, "and we can eat some of that food Tía Inez packed for us, Marshal. We need to talk about a little problem."

"Not so little, I don't think," Jenks said. "I saw that odd-looking black-and-white pony tied up back there. Do you reckon those two Johnston boys are going to try to pay you fellas back for their brother getting killed?"

"I'm afraid they may be planning to try us," Henry said, looking disgusted. "We'll have to be ready for a fight any-time now. That's the main reason I wanted to stop, to make sure we're all thinking the same way. I want the girl to get in-side the wagon. I think it's possible they might try to pick her off first, especially if Devereaux happens to be with them."

"Do you really think Devereaux could be around here? I followed him past Coffeyville and over east into the Osage country before I lost his trail, Henry. I don't think he'd be back here. He's got to know we'll eventually be taking the girl to St. Louis to her father."

"My brother disagrees with you, Marshal. Don't you, Dan?"

Dan dismounted and joined the two men. "Don't I what?"

"The Marshal thinks Devereaux went on to St. Louis. I just told him you thought he might be around here."

"I'm not sure I think that, but I certainly think it's possible."

"Well, I don't think Devereaux's riding with the Johnston brothers." Henry sounded convinced of what he said. "I think we'll have our troubles with him when we get closer to St. Louis. But our real concern right now is that there may be as many as three other men riding with those boys.

"A lot of the fellas that hang around Ma Hainey's place are nothing but no-account drifters, and some are just plain lowdown, sorry, and mean. I'm afraid any of them could be talked into joining those boys in a raid on us. There probably ain't a one of them that wouldn't do almost anything to get their hands on our horses and supplies. If we're attacked out in the open by five men, we'll have ourselves a real problem."

"We'll be all right if we're careful. You'll be driving and Marshal Jenks will take your place riding ahead of the wagon until we stop for the night, so I'll ride where Anne Marie rode earlier, a little behind the wagon. We'll all keep our eyes and ears open."

"Your brother just mentioned that the girl might be in some danger, Dan, and I think he's right. I kinda agree with what Henry just said. If that Devereaux tries anything it will be somewhere near St. Louis, but we shouldn't take any chances on that. Tell the girl to get inside the wagon and stay there—tie her horse to the tailgate where mine was."

"She's sure not going to like that," Dan grinned and shook his head.

"She don't have to like it. Can she shoot?"

"Sure she can. I taught her myself."

"Give her a long gun, Dan. Tell her to keep watch and if she sees anybody coming up behind us to fire over their heads."

"That might help, Marshal. I don't know why I have to do all the dirty jobs, though. She's going to be plumb aggravated."

"Oh, for cat's sake," Henry shook his head in exasperation, "you don't have to tell her. I'll talk to her myself after we eat. Come on, I'm hungry—even if nobody else is."

Tying the horses' reins to a tree branch to keep them away from the spring, Dan went to the back of the wagon to help Bryce down. Anne Marie stood at the tailgate, holding Bryce in her arms. "I heard what you said. No one has to tell me to ride in the wagon. You needn't fuss yourself about it."

"Don't be angry, Anne Marie, please—I didn't mean anything. I said that for Henry's benefit, is all. He's all the time thinking he's the boss."

"You made me sound like a silly child."

"Please don't take it that way." Dan looked stunned at her reaction. He stared at her scowling face, absently twisting the end of the rope that held the wagon canvas in place.

Anne Marie finally shook her head and smiled up at Dan. "I forgive you, I know you didn't mean anything. Let's go eat and get back on the road."

Dan grabbed the basket of food from the back of the wagon and followed her. They sat in a circle on a ground-sheet Henry unrolled on the grass. Anne Marie passed out the food and gave each of the men a napkin, a fork, and a tin pie plate. The basket held thin-sliced ham and fried chicken, loaves of homemade bread, a large bowl of thin-sliced potatoes flavored with bacon and pickles and two kinds of pie.

"It's hard to beat Tía Inez' cooking," Henry said as he reached for a third piece of chicken.

"There's enough here for our supper, if some people don't try to be complete hogs."

"You've got a lot of room to talk, Dan Smithson. I saw you take that third piece of apple pie."

"That's not true, Henry, I only had two pieces. You're telling tales to cover your own hoggishness."

Anne Marie looked over at Dan and laughed. "Did you say hoggishness? I don't think that's really a word."

"Well that's what Henry is, a doggone hog."

Marshal Jenks wiped his mouth with his bandanna and stood up. "If you two boys will stop bickering like you're about ten years old, we should get this basket packed up and get moving. If those Johnston boys decide to ride down on us I'd rather be in a better place than this."

"You're right about that. I'll go water the horses." Dan stood up and walked over to untie the saddle horses and lead them to the spring to drink. "I'm gonna water the team where they are. I don't want to unhook them from the wagon. It takes too long."

Dan filled a leather bucket several times to let the horses drink their fill. When he finished he returned the bucket to its hook on the side of the wagon. By that time Anne Marie and Henry had returned the leftover food to the basket, rerolled the ground sheet and packed everything back in the wagon.

Marshal Jenks dug under the wagon seat to pull out an extra Winchester and a coach gun. He checked both weapons carefully, making sure they were fully loaded. Without speaking he passed the Winchester back through the wagon to Anne Marie. He reached down to hand Henry a handful of shells for the coach gun and placed the loaded weapon on the wagon seat. Climbing back down to the ground, he motioned for Henry to get on the seat and take his turn driving.

Dan tied the extra horses behind the wagon and followed, walking his horse. The miles passed slowly. The road still ran on high ground, and they made good time. It was late afternoon when some clouds blew in from the northwest, the sky swiftly darkened and it started to rain. Dan urged his horse closer to the back of the wagon and reached behind him to grab his slicker and pull it over his head.

He could see Anne Marie sitting close to the opening in the canvas. She held the Winchester with its barrel protruding from the tailgate. The rain changed almost immediately from a sprinkle to a downpour. Rain blew against his face and clouded his vision.

Suddenly, Anne Marie fired the Winchester. Dan barely heard the report of the rifle over the downpour, but he saw the muzzle flash. He leaned against his saddle horn and looked back over his shoulder. Covering his eyes with one hand he could make out a group of riders close behind them in the gloom. The leader rode a black horse with flashes of white.

Lifting the rawhide loop that held his handgun in its holster with his left hand, he eased the pistol around and shot through his slicker at the leader. The shot missed, but the riders slowed their horses and fell back, losing themselves in the pouring rain.

When Dan turned back forward, Anne Marie disappeared from the opening in the wagon canvas. Evidently she had crawled forward to warn Henry and Marshal Jenks, because the wagon lurched forward suddenly, picking up speed. Dan spurred his horse to a fast trot to keep close behind. Turning frequently to look over his shoulder, he couldn't see anyone following. It never occurred to him that either he or Anne Marie hit anyone, but the shots gave the group of men warning that they were ready.

Those fellas probably decided they'd be well off to wait until they find a better place to get close to us.

After about twenty minutes of lurching and bumping

along the road, the wagon turned off into a clump of sycamores and cedars that Dan recognized. They'd made it to Fall River. This was the place where they talked about spending the night. The trees and bushes grew thick and heavy and would offer them some cover. He remembered that there were some banks of shelf rock somewhere close by. They'd make a good place for them to fort up.

Jumping to the ground, Dan untied the extra horses and led them around to the front of the wagon. Marshal Jenks and Henry were busy unhooking the horses from the wagon. Rain pounded down, making every movement an effort.

Dan grabbed the reins of Marshal Jenks' mount and led all the horses deep into the woods, close against the rocky bank. He tied the horses individually to low bushes in a place where he felt they'd be safe from stray bullets and where they couldn't easily be driven away if one of the Johnstons found them. He knew that they'd be in a bad fix if the men following them ever got to their horses.

Henry led the wagon team to the same area and tied them carefully. "We'll be all right here, Dan. Help me roll the wagon over tight against these rocks. It'll almost block the opening to this little depression. If that bunch following us is who we think it is, we're gonna have a fight on our hands."

"I couldn't tell how many riders were there," Dan said, "but I saw that strange-looking black horse clear enough to know who they were."

"We're well armed, and even if all five of those men come after us, we'll be hard to get at up in this corner. You get Anne Marie and Bryce down here against the rocks where they'll be protected. I'll take the north end of the bank, back here where the opening is small. You and Marshal Jenks take the way we came in—and keep your head down."

"Gotcha, big brother. Take care and shoot straight." Dan went to the back of the wagon. Without a word Anne Marie handed Bryce down to him. The boy didn't make a sound. Anne Marie had wrapped him in a blanket and a piece of oilcloth to keep him dry. Dan held the boy in one arm and reached out to help her to the ground with the other. She put the rifle in his hand and turned around to climb down on her own.

"I filled my coat pockets with bullets. I'll stay here by the wagon and help."

"You will not," Dan said firmly. "You're gonna stay over behind that group of rocks with Bryce where you'll both be safe."

"Don't be silly, Dan. You may be glad to have my help before this is over."

"You're probably right about that, but I want you to stay where you can't get hit. I'll worry myself sick if you're over here where a stray bullet can reach you."

"I don't want to worry you." Anne Marie's shoulders drooped and she looked at the ground. "I just wanted to help. I'll stay where you want me. Here, help me pull this oilcloth across these two piles of rock, I'll sit under it and hold Bryce. You use this rifle."

"No—there's no need. I've already got two rifles. You dry it off good and keep it with you, Anne Marie, just in case."

"In case of what?"

"Just in case, that's all."

"Wait a minute, Dan." Anne Marie reached up and kissed him on his lips, then ducked under the oilcloth and refused to look at him.

Shocked for a moment, Dan shook his head and turned to rush back to the wagon. Marshal Jenks crouched in the corner created by the angle of the back of the wagon and the rock face. His rifle pointed into the darkness under the trees. The rain had eased up a little, but Dan still couldn't hear much except the splash of water and the moan of the wind.

"Those Johnston boys will know exactly where we are, don't you reckon, son?"

"I don't doubt that for a minute, Marshal. They've hunted all over this ground since they were strong enough to hold a rifle up to fire it. This country's full of game. There's everything from deer and rabbits to turkeys and all kinds of birds. I reckon that Johnston family mostly lives off what those boys can shoot, with an occasional Triangle Eight beef to break up the monotony."

"How come that Johnston family wasn't able to make its way like your pa and grandpa did? This here's fine country for raising cattle, and I noticed that you folks keep a big garden and an orchard and even grow some grain to sell."

"The Johnstons came in here years back, about the same time my grandpa did. Their grandpa, old Isaiah Johnston, and mine traded work to build their cabins and start their herds. The Johnstons got along fine as long as old Isaiah lived, but he got himself killed in one of the Indian raids when his only son wasn't more than ten or twelve years old. The boy was too young, and Isaiah's wife couldn't work the place by herself, so she sold my grandpa two sections of Johnston land, the two lying closest to Elk River.

"I heard Grandpa say that he didn't see where he needed the land at the time, but he felt sorry for the woman, left alone like she was. He had him some cash money, and it was good land, so he bought it to help her. She packed up the boy and two younger girls and went down to Coffeyville to live. The family stayed down there for almost ten years, and the place stood empty all that time."

"It's a wonder the cabin didn't fall down in all that time," Marshal Jenks said, changing position to rest his legs.

"It did get in pretty rough shape, but they patched it up. Dad offered to help them fix up some, but Johnston refused. I can just barely remember when they came back. These boys' father came past our place one day in a new wagon loaded down with supplies. He said he was going to live on the place and work it. He had his wife and the three boys with him.

"Even with the amount of land they had left, Johnston could have done fine if he'd been one to work hard. They had plenty of stock living wild in the woods and hollows after all that time, and two sections of their land borders the river. They could have raised about anything they needed on that lowland.

"This Johnston wasn't much of a worker though, not like old Isaiah. He's always taken to sitting on his porch like he does now and talking against his neighbors. He seems to hate everybody for having more than he does. My daddy and mama tried to be good neighbors to them, but it seemed like they never could get along. I can remember Dad trying several times to make friends with them."

"That's a doggone shame. Looks like Johnston's boys are cut from the same cloth."

"I reckon you're right about that, Marshal. They've probably been looking for an excuse to come after me and Henry most of their lives."

"Do you see something moving over next to that crooked sycamore?"

"Yes, I do, come to think on it," Dan said. "You've got sharp eyes."

"Wait until they get close, son—no need of wasting bullets."

"I see three men. It's probably the Johnstons and one other fella."

"You may be right about that," Jenks said, "but if they know the country another one of them may come in behind us."

"Henry's keeping watch back there. He's got good eyes, too."

A shot rang out behind them. It sounded like it came from a long distance away. Dan held his breath until he heard Henry's answering fire. The three men near the big sycamore dropped down on their stomachs and started firing at the wagon. Marshal Jenks saw one of them move, and his first shot brought a yell of anguish.

Dan fired, but his bullet went over the heads of the other two men. He crouched down and watched, waiting for one of them to move. He finally made one of the men out. He was no more than twenty feet away, close to a clump of bushes. Dan fired and the man screamed and lurched up into full view to fall back against the bushes and collapse.

In between his own and Marshal Jenks' firing, Dan could still heard the sound of Henry's rifle occasionally.

Two men were firing at them now. Evidently the man Marshal Jenks hit wasn't badly hurt. Dan held his fire, waiting for a better target. Jenks patted his arm to get his attention and backed out of his position against the rock face. "I'm going around to the other side of the wagon. I think we'll do better if we separate," he whispered. "They can see our muzzle fire as well as we can see theirs. If I can get out in the woods without them hearing me I might be able to get one of them."

"Be careful, Marshal, I've got two rifles. I'll empty one as soon as you make your move. That'll make them think we're both still firing from right here."

"Keep your head down."

Aiming on a line about twenty feet into the woods, Dan fired steadily, moving the gun barrel a few inches to the left or right after each shot. He could see muzzle flashes as the men shot back. When he emptied both rifles he realized that the wind had stopped and the rain was only a sprinkle. It was finally quiet. He listened carefully, but couldn't hear Henry's rifle.

Out of the corner of his eye Dan glimpsed Marshal Jenks bent close to the ground at the edge of the trees. He had made himself a smaller target in case the men should see him, but no one fired. Dan swiftly reloaded both rifles and took another shot at the bushes where he saw the last muzzle flash. Two rifles fired back. Keeping his head low, he began to fire a little to his right, aiming away from Jenks.

Two or three minutes passed and there were no answering shots. Puzzled, Dan fired again, shooting into the ground about twenty feet in front of the wagon to avoid hitting Jenks. Suddenly a man yelled and there was a wild crashing in the bushes behind where the attackers were lying.

"Hold your fire, Dan," Jenks called out, "I've got my hands on one of the skunks and the other one's running."

Dan scrambled under the wagon and stood up on the other side. The rain had almost stopped and he could see all the way to the edge of the wood. He still held his rifle ready.

He could hear horses running back near the road. At least one of the men was getting away. Jenks loomed up in front of him, holding a man erect by his right arm twisted high behind his back.

"This here fella's name is Ben Brady. I've seen him hanging around over in Severy City a couple of times. He's one of those old boys that likes to sit around on the store porch most days, hoping something will happen. You might know, anybody that don't have any more to do than loaf around on a store porch would eventually end up getting himself in some real trouble."

"I've seen Mr. Brady in town a time or two myself." Dan decided not to mention his fight with Brady. He couldn't tell if the marshal remembered it or not. It was easy enough to see that Brady wanted to forget about it.

"I only tried to help a neighbor, Marshal," Brady whined. "Burt Johnston told me and Scully Middleton that these here Smithson fellas done rustled a big bunch of his cows. He said they was driving 'em this way so nobody around Severy City would see and catch on to their meanness."

"Shut up with your lies, you simpleton," Jenks yanked up on Brady's arm. "Do you see any cows around here?"

"You coulda hid 'em."

"You know better than that. I'll bet a dollar them Johnston boys never said any such thing. What did they tell you?"

Brady turned his head away and refused to answer.

Marshal Jenks twisted Brady's arm higher against his back. "Don't think I'll fall for your yarns. I won't born yesterday. I'm going to turn you over to the marshal's office in Springfield for attempted murder."

"It's a long ways to Springfield, Marshal. Williard Johnston's only got a little scratch on his shoulder. He took off when you jumped out and grabbed me, but he'll be on your tail the whole way. You can figure on that. That boy's a crack shot with a rifle," Brady yelled. "I wouldn't give a busted boot for your chances of making it even halfway to Springfield. Them Johnston boys is determined to get the reward that French fella from St. Louis is offering for finding that girl you fellas kidnapped. He stopped in at Ma Hainey's place to get his shoulder tied up where one o' you skunks shot him in the back. He showed us the hole and told us all about your meanness."

"Oh, the devil—I shoulda known." Jenks turned to Dan and said, "Did you hear that? That Devereaux skunk convinced these fools that he was trying to rescue Anne Marie and take her back to St. Louis for the reward. Can you believe it?"

"I heard him. I guess Devereaux had to tell people something to get them to help him. Let's get this man tied somewhere, Marshal. I've got to go check on Henry. I haven't heard a sound from over there for much too long."

"You go on ahead and make sure he's all right," Jenks said. "I'll tie brainless here on the wagon for now. As soon as I get him tied good and tight I'll go see if Johnston took all their horses." He turned to Brady. "If he didn't you might not have to walk to Neodesha."

Jenks pushed Brady ahead of him until he reached the wagon, still holding the man's arm behind his back at an awkward angle that must have been painful. "I don't know how good a friend you are to Williard Johnston fella, but I'm making you a promise right now—the first shot he sends into this camp and you're a dead man."

Chapter Nine

Henry staggered out of his hiding place just as Dan climbed back over the wagon tongue and headed toward him. He held his jacket against his left shoulder with his right hand. When Dan reached him Henry's knees gave way. He staggered and started to fall. Throwing his arms around him, Dan held as much of his weight as he could and eased him to the ground.

"What happened to you? Let me see, Henry."

"It's just a scratch. I hit that oldest Johnston boy and thought he was dead. When I went out there to check on him he pulled a hideaway gun. He hit in my shoulder—here. Honestly— it's only a scratch."

"It looks like a lot more than a scratch to me. Be still."

Dan turned to Anne Marie, speaking quickly, "Go get that lantern that's hanging on the front of the wagon and light it. Bring it back here and get me the medicine box from under the wagon seat, too."

149

"I'm all right, Dan, for heaven's sake. Help me up and stop your infernal fussing."

"Hold yourself still, Henry. You're bleeding too much to be doing a lot of moving around. Wait 'til I get a light so we can get this tied up tight."

Anne Marie placed the lantern close to Henry's head and handed Dan a big metal box. He opened it to take out a narrow roll of white sheeting and a bottle of carbolic. "Help me get his shirt off him, Anne Marie."

Lifting Henry's left shoulder, they worked his arm out of his shirt. "Look, there's no exit wound. The bullet's still in there."

"Do you know how to take it out?" Anne Marie whispered.

"Absolutely not."

"What can we do? Look, he's fainted. I guess we moved him too much."

"I'm going to tie this pad over the hole and pull it as tight as I can until we get him to a doctor."

"Is there a doctor in Severy?"

"Lord no. There's a fella that goes as a doctor in Neodesha. I know he's famous for treating the Osage Indians. He ought to be able to take a bullet out. It's a lot closer and on our way."

"What's going on with Henry, Dan?" Marshal Jenks placed his hand on Dan's shoulder.

"He caught a small caliber bullet in his shoulder. I think I've got the bleeding under control, but he's going to need a doctor. The bullet is still in there."

"He'll need to ride in the wagon. I'll cut some poles so we can make a litter to get him over there."

"Stay here with him, Anne Marie. I'll go help Marshal Jenks make him a bed in the wagon."

Sick with worry, Dan hurriedly moved the food basket and a bag of oats forward in the wagon so he could rearrange several blankets and make a second bed on the floor.

"Missy," Jenks said, "you'll have to ride horseback at least until we reach that railroad town. We'll see how Henry is then. It might be we'll have to leave him there and pick him up on the way back."

"There'll be no leaving Henry, Marshal," Dan said. "We'll wait right there in the town with him until he's well enough to go on. Just forget about leaving him."

"Sorry, son—I didn't mean to upset you. I just thought it might take several days for him to be ready to ride again."

"I am upset, but it's not your fault. If Henry can't ride a horse he'll ride the wagon or the train until that shoulder heals. I'm not about to leave him with strangers."

Moving Henry as carefully as possible, Dan and Jenks eased him over on to the makeshift litter and carried him to the wagon. He woke up as they were settling him on the pallet in the wagon bed.

"What happened—where am I, Dan?"

"You passed out, Henry. Take it easy—I bandaged your shoulder tight enough to stop the bleeding, and we're going to take you to that Indian doctor in Neodesha. That bullet's got to come out of your shoulder."

"Thanks. It hurts, but you're right about that."

"Did Burt Johnston get away?"

"No. I killed him. I didn't really go to do it—it was sort of automatic. When he jumped up at me with that little gun in his hand, I just pulled the trigger on my rifle. The bullet caught him in the throat."

"Was he the only one that came at you?" Jenks asked.

"Yeah. Burt was definitely alone. How many were on your end?"

"Me and the marshal think they started out with three. He captured one of them, that Brady fella I had that set to with over to Severy City. I hit one other early in the fight. I think he was hard hit, by the way he acted, but we decided to wait until daylight to go looking for him."

Wary of making a fire that might make them a target, the group finished up the food left in the basket for their supper. Bryce slept in the wagon beside Henry, and Anne Marie unrolled Henry's bedroll under the wagon for her bed. Marshal Jenks took the first watch, shaking Dan's shoulder to wake him up well after midnight.

"If you get drowsy before light, wake me. Leave your brother sleep if he can. He's liable to bring on a fever from that shoulder wound, and a little extra rest might help ward it off."

Dan leaned against a tree on the edge of the small clearing and kept his eyes moving. He searched from the trees back to the pile of rocks and over the area around the wagon over and over. Everything stayed quiet. The sky gradually cleared and the moon came out bright. He could see thousands of stars. They glistened as though the rain had washed the heavens sparkling clean.

The sky had begun to lighten and show red streaks when he heard a sound beside the wagon. Marshal Jenks folded his bed and threw it across his saddle. He waved to Dan to come in and started gathering wood to make a fire. The sun was peeking over the trees when he called out, "Coffee's hot folks, come on let's get started."

Dan went down to the river to wash up and bring a bucket of fresh water for Anne Marie and Bryce to wash. As he came back up the hill he called to Marshal Jenks, "Hold up there, Marshal. I'm going to make us a real meal on this nice fire. We're not in so much of a hurry we can't take time to eat. Why don't you go on out in those bushes and see if you can figure out what happened to that fella I hit last night while I get this going. It won't take me long, and we'll travel better for a hot meal."

"I won't argue with you. This coffee is a blessing, and some bacon and bread would go down mighty fine. I noticed that girl moving about. Has she said anything to you about how Henry's feeling this morning?"

"No, but he's awake, and he sure sounded grumpy when I asked him how he felt a few minutes ago."

"Well that's nothing new."

Chuckling, Dan went to the front of the wagon and took a large wooden box from behind the seat. Balancing it on a flat rock he raised the hinged lid to remove a Dutch oven. He placed it on the fire to heat as he selected the supplies he needed.

Pouring flour, salt, soda and water into another pan, he deftly mixed the ingredients together. Pinching off good-sized balls of dough, he shaped enough biscuits to fill the oven. Replacing the lid, he found a little tin shovel and used it to fill the flat top of the lid with hot coals so the bread would brown top and bottom.

Lifting a big iron spider out of the box, he set it over the coals. Holding up a flat bundle, he unwound a white cloth from a large slab of bacon. He pulled his knife out of his boot and cut off enough thick slices to fill the pan. He also removed a Mason jar of apple jelly from the box, a stack of pie pans for plates and some forks. Then he closed it so he could use the top as a table.

The food was ready when Marshal Jenks came back to the wagon. He led a roan horse wearing a beat-up old McClellan saddle. "I found the fella you shot, Dan. He didn't make it far before he bled to death. We'll have to pack both bodies with us to that town, I reckon. They'll have someone there that can take care of them. I think this yahoo has a poster out on him. I'll check on that when we get to the town.

"Henry didn't say so before, but I reckon what he did say means he killed that fella that was shooting at him last night."

"It does."

"That's what I figured," Jenks said.

"So how many bushwhackers do we have left to worry about?"

"I'd say there's just one," Jenks answered. "That would be the last Johnston brother. I think his name is Williard. I found the tracks of two horses heading back toward the road. I'm certain that only one of them had a rider. My best guess is that those Johnston boys had Brady and this one other fella with 'em, the one you shot."

"Of course that doesn't mean the one that's left can't get more help, but I think we'll just have to watch out for Williard. He'll probably try to shoot us down from a distance. I don't think he'll leave off now. It may be that he can't, since we're responsible for both his brothers being dead," Dan said. "I think he'll follow us until he kills us or 'til one of us kills him."

"Maybe we should sit tight here for a while. I don't relish riding out in the open under Johnston's rifle, do you?"

"You've got a point, Marshal. Let's eat and we'll talk."

Dan finished eating his breakfast and helped clean up and restore the pans and other utensils to the wooden box and put it back in the wagon. Climbing under the wagon, he gathered up two extra blankets and motioned to Marshal Jenks to show him where the dead men were. The sun was high when they finished wrapping the bodies and loading them on horses.

While Jenks watered the horses and hooked the team up to the wagon Dan sat on a fallen log and carefully cleaned and reloaded his rifle. He caught his horse and tied it where it could graze in the enclosed area behind the wagon. Taking a pair of moccasins from his saddlebag, he leaned against the tailgate to remove his boots and slip the moccasins on. He picked up his rifle in his left hand.

"Give me your boots, Dan," Anne Marie reached one hand out from the back of the wagon.

Dan turned in surprise to smile at her. "I thought you and Bryce were asleep."

"I dropped off earlier while I was getting him back to sleep. I didn't get much sleep last night. We got wet and cold in those rocks and I was scared half to death."

"You don't have to be scared. We'll take care of you."

"I heard you talking. There's still one of those men trying to kill us."

"You heard right, but if you'll stay in the wagon today you'll be safe. I'm going to find him."

"Take care, please. I don't want anything to happen to you."

"Don't worry about me, you just stay in the wagon with Bryce and Henry and keep back away from this opening so Johnston can't see you."

Marshal Jenks came around the end of the wagon. He looked at Dan's moccasins and raised his eyebrows. "Are you ready to go?"

"Marshal, stay here the rest of the day, please. It'll be fairly safe here. I'm going to slip off into those woods up ahead of us. There're a lot of trees for Johnston to hide in along that trail beside the river. If we take the wagon along there now we'll be sitting ducks. I'll find Johnston and make sure it's safe for us to go on."

"Who elected you?"

"I did. I'm the best person for the job, so leave it alone."

Without saying another word, Dan turned his back on Jenks and walked swiftly into the trees. Jenks stood still and watched the spot Dan disappeared to for a few minutes, a blank expression on his face. He finally shrugged his shoulders and turned to find a seat on a log near the wagon, resting his rifle across his knees.

Sun sparkled on the wet trees and grass along the edges of the track. The swollen river had raged out of its banks in several low places. Small rivulets of the muddy water ran across the roadway, but none seemed large enough to impede travel.

Dan found the trail of Johnston's horse as soon as he reached the road. The tracks dug deep for about a mile, indicating the horse was running hard. Johnston was headed south along the river. Dan followed at a jog, knowing Johnston would have to ease his pace soon, because a horse couldn't run long in mud.

When the road turned away from the river a little, the tracks became lighter. It was like Dan had figured. Johnston had started walking his horse. After a while Dan came to a jumble of tracks. It looked like Johnston had stopped and turned the horse around several times.

He probably started running in a panic, then when he calmed down he stopped here to think about what he wanted to do.

Circling the jumble of tracks several times, Dan found where the horse left the road. Its tracks headed west into a clump of buckhorn and sedge mixed in with scrub trees. Crouching to make as small a target as possible, he carefully slid between the limbs of two small sycamores and stood still to get his bearings.

He listened carefully in case the man might be somewhere near. Searching the ground, he spotted another track left by Johnston's horse and advanced slowly, putting each foot down slowly, taking care not to make a sound.

Dan heard a snuffling sound and a heavy step. Sure he would be seen, he jumped behind a tree and stood still, his rifle ready. Taking a moment to catch his breath, he leaned forward and looked around the bole of the tree in the direction of the sounds. The white on the rump of the black horse was visible through the foliage.

Maybe Johnston decided to wait here for us here. I'll have to get closer to find out exactly where he is.

Five careful steps later, he was close enough to see the entire body of the horse. Johnston wasn't anywhere in sight.

The horse sensed Dan and nickered as he turned to face him. It almost seemed to Dan that the animal was glad to see him. He jumped behind another tree and froze. If Johnston happened to be anywhere within hearing distance he would know exactly where to find him.

When nothing happened, Dan lifted his rifle and charged into the small clearing. The horse half reared and jumped back in alarm, almost pulling its reins loose from the tree limb where he was tied. Johnston wasn't there. Dan instantly understood what had happened. Johnston hid the horse and circled back near the road to lie in wait for their wagon.

The low-down murdering skunk—I missed him somehow, but I'll find him.

Whirling, he ran back the way he came until he reached the edge of the woods. Staying a little away from the road, under cover of the bushes he worked his way back north, still careful to move quietly. After about two hundred yards he found Johnston's boot prints headed north on a track parallel to the road. The prints looked like they were fresh.

Dan advanced slowly, expecting to find Johnston lying in wait for the wagon at any moment. He put his hand on the bole of a stunted oak and touched mud. Johnston had climbed the tree. He was just overhead. Crouching, Dan backed away and looked up, his rifle ready. The tree was empty. He looked around for tracks and found the impression of a pair of boots that dug deep in the soft ground.

Maybe he climbed up and tried to see back down the road. He surely gave it up, if that's what he did, 'cause here's where he jumped down from there and went on walking.

Alternately watching the ground and the trees, Dan continued to follow Johnston's trail. When the brush began to open up and the trees got larger he realized that he was almost back to where they'd been attacked the night before. Thankful the others were willing to stay forted up instead of traveling, he moved forward slowly, watching for any movement.

Suddenly he heard a rifle boom. It was ahead and above him. Johnston had climbed a tree again and was firing at the others at the wagon. Angry and afraid, Dan took several more steps toward the sound, frantically searching the limbs of nearby trees for his quarry.

Marshal Jenks bent to drop an armful of wood on the fire just as a bullet sang past his head. He fell to the ground and rolled back behind the wagon. Grabbing a rifle, he fired back toward the trees in the direction the shot came from.

Anne Marie called from the wagon, "Are you all right, Marshal?"

"Yes. He missed me—scared me witless—but he missed me."

"Well, keep your head down, for goodness sake. Maybe that shot will help Dan find the man."

"I'm almighty thankful we decided to stay here," Jenks said. "I think we'd be fools to keep moving with somebody hiding out there and shooting at us. We'll just sit tight where we are for a few more hours. Dan'll get Johnston and come on back to the wagon eventually."

Jenks lay under the wagon holding his rifle ready, but nothing happened. About an hour later he heard Dan call. "Don't shoot. I've got Johnston and I'm coming in."

Marshal Jenks reached Dan first. He followed Williard Johnston into camp with his rifle aimed at the middle of his back. Without saying a word Jenks grabbed Johnston by the arm and, leading him to the wagon, tied him to the spokes of one of the wheels. Johnston fought the ropes for a moment then gave up to slide down to sit in the mud with his hands pulled up in the air over his head.

Anne Marie jumped down from the wagon and ran to meet Dan. "I don't know when I was ever so glad to see anyone. Sitting here and waiting had to be one of the hardest things I ever had to do. What took you so long?"

Dan smiled down at her without answering.

"Come to the wagon," she said softly, smiling back. "Henry's awake and wants to talk to you."

Dan stepped to the end of the wagon and looked in at his brother.

Henry raised his head to say, "Where've you been so long?"

"I didn't waste any time. You do the hunting next time if you think you can do it any faster."

The marshal stepped up beside Dan. "Come on now, boys. Cut out the arguing for once in your lives. Dan's trying to tell us how he caught the polecat."

"I'll tell you. I was close to him when I heard him shoot. I trailed him first and found where he left his horse, then turned back along the west side of the road. It took him a while and he climbed up several trees and waited for you to come on down the road until he realized you'd stayed forted up right here.

"The sound of that shot like to scared me to death. Williard Johnston's been hunting since he was no bigger'n a gnat. I didn't expect him to miss. The only thing I can think is that he got too anxious and didn't allow for shooting down on you like that. I was some kind of glad to see you stand up when I came in. I could see Anne Marie looking out the end of the wagon almost as soon as you yelled.

"Johnston concentrated so hard on getting a bead on somebody here in camp that I was able to creep up and get my gun right on him. I spotted him sitting straddle on a low limb on that big old oak tree out there about a hundred yards to your left.

"I got around behind the tree and pulled myself up on another limb and got settled. Just about the time Johnston raised his rifle to get off another shot, I reached up and stuck the barrel of my rifle right in his ribs. He must have been so intent on shooting one of you, he couldn't even hear me moving."

"I can't hardly believe it's all over." Marshal Jenks took his pipe out of his mouth. "It seems like about a week since last night."

"You're right about that," Dan said. "Could we just stay here and relax until early tomorrow, or do you think we should go on now?"

"Let's go on, son. I think we've got time to make it to that town before night. I'd like to get Henry to that doctor and find out about the train to Springfield. I don't know how often they run a train through there that passengers can ride."

Without a word, Dan began to get the horses ready. As he worked, he noticed with pride that Anne Marie left the wagon unasked to throw a bucket of water on the fire and scatter the black coals. Then she took Bryce and disappeared into the brush. After a few minutes she returned and helped Bryce climb over the tailgate, then without a word she followed him into the wagon.

That girl mighta been born to a different kinda life, but she'll make me a perfect ranch wife.

Marshal Jenks untied Johnston from the wagon wheel, but

kept his hands tied together. He jerked him forward to help him up on one of the horses that were hitched to the wagon. He tied a rope on one of Johnston's ankles and ran it under the horse's belly to fasten it to his other leg. Yanking his arms out in front of him, he tied Johnston's hands firmly to the top of his mount's collar.

"You can't do this. I can't ride on top of this harness like this, it'll kill me. I'll never make it to Neodesha."

"Sorry fella—you'll have to make it. This is the best I can do."

"I could ride behind Brady there. His horse can carry double." Brady gave Johnston a dirty look.

Marshall Jenks shook his head. He actually smiled at Johnston. "I said no."

"I'll get you for this, Jenks."

"I don't think so," Jenks said. "I think you've about done all the mischief you're going to do. At least for a long, long time."

Cursing vilely, Johnston continued to scream all of the dire things he planned to do to Marshal Jenks and the Smithson brothers. Finally disgusted with the man's foul language, Dan rode up beside Johnston and swatted him across the back of his head with his hat.

"Shut up you—just shut the dickens up. I've had enough of your filthy mouth. If you say another word I'll cut you loose and make you walk to Neodesha behind my horse—with a new rope around your neck."

Johnston didn't say anything else. He dropped his head until it almost touched the top of the horse's harness. He moaned his discomfort when Dan signaled for the wagon to stop so he could go in the woods and retrieve Johnston's paint horse.

"This horse is all rested, Marshal. Do you think we could

transfer Johnston over to ride him? I expect sitting on that roach-backed gelding with all that leather underneath him is considerably uncomfortable."

"I don't want him moved," Jenks said. "He'd not thank us. He'd just use the opportunity to try to get away. I say leave him sit exactly where he is. If the harness hurts his rump it's no more'n what he deserves."

Neodesha nestled close to where the Fall and the Verdigris Rivers ran together. Osage Indians settled there first, and then whites moved in and took over. Some of them were trappers from Montreal who married Osage women. The town looked like any other east Kansas settlement until you noticed the curved corners and other decorations on the roof of some of the oldest houses. You could also hear a French sounding name here and there.

The town boasted a combination pastor and schoolteacher. He arranged for the burial of Burt Johnston and the other man. The other man turned out to be an escaped prisoner from somewhere in Illinois. The town constable offered Jenks the use of a stout log smokehouse to incarcerate Williard Johnston and Brady while they were in town. The marshal studied the little building for a while and finally decided to take him up on his offer, but he left Johnston's and Brady's hands and feet tied and slept the night through leaning back against the door of the little building with his rifle across his knees.

They found the doctor and he dug the bullet out of Henry's shoulder. Henry argued that they should go on by wagon the next morning, not wait for the train, but Dan refused. He made arrangements for Henry to have a bed in the doctor's infirmary. He wanted him to take time to rest and heal.

Asking around, he found a good campsite in a grove of trees near the river where they could wait. The next train wasn't due to come through for three days. No matter how much Henry argued about it, Dan was determined to give him that long to rest.

"I've made arrangements to leave the wagon and horses at the livery when we catch the train," Dan explained to Marshal Jenks. "Boarding horses can get expensive, so I made a deal with the fella that owns the livery. He needs to haul about a ton of grain some place about twenty miles downriver, so he's going to use our wagon and team while we're gone in return for keeping our horses. We figured that doing it that way, neither one of us will be out any money."

"Did you tell Henry about that?"

"Lord no," Dan said, rolling his eyes, "he'd have five different ideas of what we should do. He's about frantic to get out here and boss this trip as it is. I just went ahead and took care of things without telling him anything."

"I'm thankful he's well enough to be talking like he was this morning, aren't you?"

"Of course I am," Dan said, "but I still say he's bound to be in a fret that he can't be out here with us."

"I reckon you're right about that," Jenks said. "He'll be sitting up a little by tomorrow, I'll bet. The doctor said that as long as he didn't work up a fever, he'd heal fast."

"How much farther is it to Springfield?"

"Somewhere in the neighborhood of eighty miles. I reckon the train will make a few stops on the way, but the filthy thing's sure faster than a wagon and we'll be about ten times safer if that Devereaux is anywhere around."

"Let's get a fire going so we can cook some supper."

Chapter Ten

Dirt and soot covered the train windows. The tied-back curtains and horsehair on the seats smelled of stale tobacco. The ride was uncomfortable, tedious, and slow. It seemed as though the train made a stop every hour, either at another small town or to take on wood or water.

Henry and Marshal Jenks had stayed close behind Henry as he climbed aboard, but he refused their help and found a seat alone, insisting he felt fine. Anne Marie changed from her riding clothes into a dress and coat she and Inez had made for her from Dan and Henry's mother's clothes. She almost jumped with excitement when they came aboard. She had never ridden a train before. Dan had never been on a train before either, but he wasn't impressed.

"This shore ain't much of a improvement over a wagon is it?" Dan asked, smiling down at Anne Marie. "Are you tired?"

"No—no thank you, I'm not tired. I'm too excited to settle down."

"Are you feeling anxious to get home?" Dan asked softly, sounding apprehensive.

"I'm excited about seeing new things and going new places. I think I'm sort of mixed up about going home. I want to go, don't get me wrong, but I don't want to leave you."

Turning in the seat, Dan reached for her hand and leaned close to whisper, "I don't want you to go, either, but there's no other way."

"If you could stay in St. Louis a few days, I could see Father—let him know I'm all right—and turn around and come back with you." She raised her hand to her mouth as she said, "Would you like that?"

"I'd like to turn around right now and take you home with me, but we're being silly."

"I'm not being silly."

"You have to go home, Anne Marie, there's no other way."

"I know, but I'm afraid of how it will be. I really don't want be Anne Marie Devereaux again; I'd rather be your wife."

"After you go home to your father," Dan said sternly. He turned his head and got up to move to another seat to signal the end of the conversation.

Anne Marie stuck close to Marshal Jenks when they left the train in Springfield. It wasn't far to the hotel, but Dan hailed one of the buckboard drivers waiting at the depot and let Jenks help Anne Marie, Bryce, and Henry aboard while he gathered up their baggage and baskets and threw them in the back.

He paid the buckboard driver extra to wait where he was while he hailed another buckboard. He and Marshal Jenks went back in the car and unclasped the leg-irons that held their prisoners secure to the legs of one of the seats. They pushed and shoved the two men outside and up into the rear seat of waiting buckboard.

After dropping Johnston and Brady off at the Springfield town jail to await their trial, Marshal Jenks went to the Federal Marshal's Office to wire some reports to Fort Smith. He had announced when they left the station that he'd take care of that business and stay overnight with a friend instead of going to the hotel. The rest of the group checked in at the drovers' hotel. They planned to take a few days rest at the hotel while they waited for Marshal Jenks to complete his business.

Over Dan's protests Henry left him with Anne Marie and Bryce on the porch of the hotel to walk to the telegraph office. During the train ride he and Jenks had composed a telegram to send to Julian Devereaux at Château d'Arc plantation. They had drafted another that the marshal would send to the Town Marshal's Office in St Louis.

Henry and Dan had argued about what to do about notifying Devereaux, but finally agreed it would be too much of a shock for a sick man if they just walked in on him with Anne Marie. They also knew that if they ran into trouble with Anne Marie's uncle they would need the cooperation of the local law.

Dan escorted Anne Marie and Bryce into the hotel and engaged their rooms. He helped Anne Marie take her bags and Bryce up to her room then went back downstairs to get his pack and Henry's. When he got back upstairs to his room he dropped the things on the bed and started back to the door, planning on finding some place to get a cold beer. About the time he touched the knob someone knocked.

When he opened the door Anne Marie stood there. She

had removed her traveling coat and wore the blue dress. She had taken time to wash her face and brushed her hair. Dan's heart started pounding. She smiled up at him, looking amazingly fresh and beautiful.

"Anne Marie—you startled me. Is anything wrong with your room?"

"Oh—no, it's nothing like that. The room is surprisingly nice. Bryce is sound asleep, and I wondered if you would go downstairs to the dining room with me."

"I'd like that. Let's go."

When Henry came back to the hotel he stopped at the desk for his key and looked through the dining room doorway. Dan and Anne Marie sat on the same side of one of the tables with coffee cups in front of them. Their smooth dark heads almost touched. Dan held one of Anne Marie's hands in both of his.

Henry shook his head and muttered to himself, "That boy's going to get hurt bad and there's not a blasted thing I can do about it." He continued to stand and watch Dan and Anne Marie whisper to each other for a moment, then turned away to go upstairs.

They stayed in Springfield two full days, spending most of their time resting. Henry kept to himself, claiming he needed the rest because of his swiftly healing wound. Several times he volunteered to watch over Bryce so Dan and Anne Marie could have time alone together. Around noon on the second day, Marshal Jenks knocked on Henry's door, announcing that his business was complete and he was ready to go on to St. Louis.

"When's the next train out of this burg?" Henry asked, waving Jenks to a seat on the room's lone chair. He flopped back down on the bed. "I'm so tired of this hotel room and minding that overgrown baby I could yell or something."

"Where's the rest of the family?"

"They're downstairs getting something to eat. I've been trying to make myself scarce so Dan and that girl can have a chance to talk."

"I'm glad to hear that, Henry. I could see they were about as took with one another as you and that Bella Slade are."

"I guess you're right about that."

"If you feel up to it, let's walk on down to the station and check the schedule," Jenks said as he stood up and put his hat on. "The fresh air'll probably do you good. I think there's a train leaving here early tomorrow morning that goes almost straight through to St. Louis. It'll be a sight better trip than that run-in from Kansas was. You can bet on that."

"That'll certainly be a help. I don't know when I ever saw anything as dirty, stinking, or aggravating as that doggone train."

Marshal Jenks looked at Henry and laughed as he said, "You ain't traveled much, have you, son?"

Henry smiled at Jenks and led the way downstairs. When they reached the station they found that Jenks was correct; there was an express with two passenger cars that left early the next day. They purchased tickets for everybody and hurried back to the hotel to tell the Dan and Anne Marie to get ready for an early morning departure.

Dan sat across from Anne Marie on the train. He felt a glow of happiness every time he looked at her. The feeling always melted into a wave of sadness. He knew it would only be a short time before she would go back to her true life as the only daughter of a wealthy plantation owner. That life would have no room for a half-educated hick from east Kansas.

He argued to himself that he was a lot better off than most men were. He would own half the Triangle Eight in less than two years, with half their herd of cattle and somewhere in the neighborhood of fifty fine horses.

It was nothing to sneeze at by any standard, but he knew a six-room ranch house made out of part rip-sawed clapboards and part log cabin couldn't compare with the poorest kind of plantation house. He couldn't help but fear that once Anne Marie returned home, she'd find someone else, someone more like her father.

The train arrived in St. Louis late in the evening. As they left the car, Marshal Jenks said, "I know a Mrs. Perkins that runs a boardinghouse right down the street here, and she sets the best table in this town. Her place'll be perfect for you folks unless you particularly want to go to a hotel."

"That sounds fine, Jenks," Henry said.

"Come on then, I'll walk down there with you and introduce you."

Jenks led them directly to Mrs. Perkins' house. She had rooms available so they engaged them. Marshal Jenks resolved to take his meals with them at the boardinghouse, but to rent a room at a small hotel down the street. He didn't even ask for a room, knowing Mrs. Perkins wouldn't welcome him—that she'd be afraid he might decide to arrest someone, perhaps even one of her boarders and cause a disturbance in her place.

When Mrs. Perkins heard Anne Marie's story she offered the services of her maid to help her get her dresses unpacked and pressed so she could be properly dressed when she went out to her father's plantation the next day. The group ate the sumptuous dinner their landlady prepared and went to bed early.

Rested and dressed in their best clothes, the entire party set out early the next morning to make the ten-mile trip to Château d'Arc. Dan drove a hired buggy and Anne Marie sat close beside him. They whispered together the whole way. Henry sat in the rear seat and held Bryce on his knee. Marshal Jenks rode on horseback beside the buggy.

"You know you have to stay with your father, Anne Marie," Dan said. "I'm not going to run away with you."

"You lied when you said you loved me. If you really loved me you wouldn't do this to me."

"I do so love you and you know it. If you love me like you say you do you'll stop this, it's not fair. You know you've got to go home—and it's got nothing to do with me. You heard your uncle say your father's ill."

"I want to see my father, but I don't want you to leave me. Suppose he won't let me keep Bryce with me. He may not understand how I feel about him."

"Don't go making up problems, girl. Your father won't do that—stop borrowing trouble. We need to take this one thing at a time. I'll be of age in less than two years, and you'll be almost twenty by then. That'll give us a better chance."

"I wish I hadn't worn this dress," Anne Marie said, her voice full of tears, "I'd rather ride." She turned her head away and moved to the other side of the seat, as far away from Dan as she could get.

The road out of St. Louis ran close beside the river. As he drove south Dan admired the carefully mown fields filled with sleek, fat horses and small bunches of cattle, some that looked very different from the range cattle he was used to seeing.

When he turned the buggy between two brick pillars marked Château d'Arc and caught sight of the main house through a grove of trees, Dan's heart sank like a stone. The Triangle Eight house—his home—was smaller than the gatehouse. He looked down at Anne Marie with dismay on his face.

She looked uncomfortable and her voice sounded harsh. "Stop looking at me like that. I'd honestly forgotten how big this place is. Please Dan—I'm not that house."

"You'll be living in a world that's so far above me and mine you'll forget all about me in a week."

"Just shut up—please—please shut up. Don't do this to me. I'm no different than I was on the trail, or in Springfield, or back in Kansas. I'll still be Anne Marie Devereaux—still me, no matter how big my father's house is. And I'll still love you."

A black man came out of the double doors of the tall brick house the instant Dan stopped the buggy. He pushed a dark-haired man in a wheelchair. Anne Marie gasped and jumped down from the wagon without waiting for Dan's help and ran up the steps to kneel at the feet of the man in the wheelchair.

"Poppa—oh, Poppa. You're better. You're out of bed. I'm so glad, I believed you were dying."

"Anne Marie—I'd given you up. Let me look at you . . . you're as tall as your mother was. You've grown up. You're not my little girl any longer."

"I'll always be your little girl, Poppa." Anne Marie struggled to laugh with tears running down her cheeks.

"Here, Poppa, let me introduce my friends. Meet Marshal Jenks and Henry Smithson and his brother Dan Smithson—he's the one driving the team. Dan is the man who rescued me—actually he rescued me twice."

"How do you do, gentlemen. I am greatly in your debt." Julian Devereaux sketched a bow from his chair.

"Anne Marie, you didn't introduce the handsome young man staring at me from the back of the buggy."

"Oh, Poppa. This is Bryce Gillis. He's my little brother. Not actually my brother, of course, but I take care of him. He's my responsibility."

"Well, I do say. You obviously have a lot to tell me, my dear. Invite your friends in for something cool to drink."

Anne Marie went back to the buggy to help Bryce get his toys together.

Julian Devereaux turned to address Dan. "Will you men be staying in St. Louis long, Mr. Smithson?"

Dan climbed down from the buggy and walked up the steps to face Devereaux before he answered. "We only came to see that Anne Marie got home all right, Mr. Devereaux, and to make sure you knew about everything that's happened so you can keep her safe."

"What do you mean by that, young man?" Devereaux looked and sounded annoyed.

"We've got proof that your brother Andre was responsible for your daughter's kidnapping—that he paid a man named Gillis to steal your daughter. She says he ordered him to kill her. Your brother found out recently that Anne Marie was still alive and he hunted Gillis down and murdered him. Then he tried to kill Anne Marie. When he failed, he put a price on her head that sent a group of low-down loafers to chase her for the reward."

Devereaux lifted his head proudly and looked annoyed. "Mr. Smithson, I'm sure you are mistaken. My brother is right here in St. Louis as we speak. He sustained a serious wound several weeks ago when fighting Indians over in Kansas somewhere. He came home to recuperate. He's staying in my own townhouse."

"Mr. Devereaux, we thought you might have a hard time believing that your own brother would do you so much dirt, so we brought you copies of the letters he wrote to Gillis. Gillis saved them and tried to use them to blackmail more money out of him. Anne Marie can tell you how your brother and his men attacked our house and tried to kill her. Marshal Jenks here was there, too, and can vouch for the whole story."

"Mr. Smithson, you must admit this is a wild story. You expect me to believe that my only brother paid this Gillis person to steal my daughter and kill her? This is a fantastic charge, sir, it's crazy."

Dan held out a roll of papers. "Here're the copies of your brother's letters to Raoul Gillis, sir. The one's he tried to blackmail him with." He raised his voice, his tone clearly expressed his aggravation with Devereaux's attitude. "You not only have these letters to tell the story, but your own daughter will tell you that Gillis took her away from her school and forced her to stay with him.

"She heard Gillis tell his wife that your brother instructed him to kill her, and she saw your brother's face when he grabbed her and tried to steal her out of my house. He gave me this fresh scar here on my temple, and I put that bullet in his back as he ran away from me."

"Please do not shout at me, young man," Devereaux said. He stiffened at Dan's words and turned his head away, refusing to look at him.

Anne Marie ran back to kneel beside her father's wheelchair. "Poppa, you must believe Dan—and me. Uncle Andre broke into the Smithsons' house and knocked Dan out with a pistol. He wounded their housekeeper and dragged me away, raving that he would to kill me. Dan chased after him and saved me. Please—you must believe us. If it weren't for Dan and his family I'd be dead."

Devereaux's face paled and his voice shook. "I can't take this in. It's too much." He looked up at Dan. "I've instructed the manager of Wells Fargo in St. Louis to pay you the reward for finding my daughter."

Dan shouted, disgust in his voice, and Henry repeated after him, "We didn't bring Anne Marie home to collect any reward."

"You're entitled to the reward. I posted it the first month after my daughter disappeared. Why are you men so angry?"

Dan put one hand on Anne Marie's shoulder and looked down at her father. "You don't understand much at all, Mr. Devereaux. Some of us do things for people because it's the right thing to do, not for money. I'll speak plain. Your brother wants Anne Marie dead. We're not leaving her here if you don't do something about him so she'll be safe."

Julian Devereaux threw back his head and stared into Dan's eyes. His voice was icy. "No one speaks to me like that young man."

Dan leaned forward to plead, "I don't mean to be disrespectful, sir. I love your daughter and I'm afraid for her."

"You say you love my daughter? Why you back-woods pup—how dare you. Get out of here. Get off my property."

"I'm not going to leave Anne Marie in danger." Dan held his head high and shouted back at Devereaux, "I don't care what you say. I believe your brother is determined to kill her. I think he'll stop at nothing to do it."

Devereaux lowered his head and put one hand over his eyes. "I'm ill," he said softly. "This is all more than I can stand. I must rest now. Anne Marie, you'll be safe in this house—you know you will. I'll read these letters and I won't let Andre come to the château." He raised his head and looked up at Dan. "Is that enough for you, Mr. Smithson?"

"Not really. I'll wait here until you read your brother's letters, Mr. Devereaux. I'm sure you'll recognize his handwriting. I'll want them back when you finish. I want the authorities in St. Louis to have copies. I believe that once they read them and hear what we have to say they'll arrest your brother for kidnapping and attempted murder."

"You can't be serious? You would sully my family's name by taking these letters to the authorities? You must understand, young man, in my class we handle our own affairs, we do not take our differences to law."

Devereaux turned to the tall black man standing beside the door. "Joshua, go get one of your sons and escort Mr. Smithson and company to the front gate."

Marshal Jenks dismounted and walked up the steps to stand beside Dan. "Don't get yourself too upset now, Devereaux. I can back up everything this boy said to you. I agree with them about the danger to your daughter. I'm not leaving the child here until something is done about your brother."

"Marshal, my brother Andre's my only family except for my daughter. What do you expect me to do? This story cannot be true. I cannot believe it."

"I expect you to see sense, man," Jenks' voice rose and he sounded impatient. "Your brother paid a man to kidnap your only child and murder her. When he found out the man kept the child alive he followed him to Kansas and killed him. Once Gillis was out of the way he hunted Anne Marie down and tried to grab her. He swore he'd bring her back here and kill her in front of you. That's gospel— you've got to accept it."

"There's other papers in this basket, Mr. Devereaux," Dan said. "Maybe a look at them will help you to believe."

"What sort of papers are they?"

"There're some deeds and a family bible. The best I can make out, the deeds are for properties in this area—here they are. The Bible is for the family of another Julian Devereaux. Anne Marie said it belonged to Gillis' wife."

"My God. I just recently found out that these deeds were missing. Most of them are the only proof that I hold title to some small properties I purchased several years ago. The last time I saw them they were in my office.

"I recently had occasion to look for them and couldn't find them. I convinced myself that the deeds weren't lost, that I had put them in the hands of my lawyer. I planned to ask him about them the next time I visited his office. The Julian Devereaux in this Bible is my own grandfather. Gillis' wife was a distant cousin."

"Mr. Devereaux," Marshal Jenks said, "I don't know what Raoul Gillis or your brother planned exactly, but it's plain he wants this property, and he wants it any way he can get it. He's waiting for you to die and expects to make sure he inherits."

Devereaux dropped his head into his hands. "You have to be mistaken, Marshal. It cannot be true. There has to be another explanation."

"I'm sorry to put this on you, sir, you being sick and all, but I agree with Smithson here. Anne Marie can't be left here until Andre Devereaux is dead or behind bars."

"How can you say this? Anne Marie, you wouldn't leave with these people?"

"Poppa, these men are telling you the truth. If you won't believe them I'll have to go back to Kansas with them."

"My God. I'll read the letters. Please wait, Marshal Jenks—I'll read the letters and then give them to you to do what you think best with them."

He turned to Anne Marie. "If I tell the marshal how to find Andre and promise to keep Joshua and his three sons on guard around the house will you stay here with me?"

"Yes, Poppa. I'll stay. As long as you accept that what we're telling you is the truth, I know you'll keep me safe."

Smiling, Anne Marie turned to Dan. "Is that all right? I've known Joshua and his sons all my life. They'll stop Uncle Andre if he tries to hurt me."

"I don't like it, Anne Marie," Dan said, reaching for her hands. "Will you promise me that you'll stay in the house where you'll be safe until we get the authorities to take your uncle into custody?"

"I promise. Cross my heart. Oh, Dan, please understand—

I really do want to stay with my father. I'll think about you all the time, I promise, but now that I'm here I want to stay."

Marshal Jenks sat on the edge of the porch and waited while Devereaux read the packet of letters. Henry helped Dan unload Anne Marie and Bryce's bags, then sat on the step to play with Bryce while they waited. Anne Marie stood beside her father's chair.

When he finished reading, Devereaux rolled the letters and handed them back to Jenks. "Marshal, if I accept all that you and my daughter tell me and add it to what I read here I must believe that my brother is all that you say. I have to admit, this hurts me almost as much as it did to lose my daughter."

"I'm sorry, Mr. Devereaux. I reckon it must be awful hard to swallow."

"Hard to swallow," Devereaux repeated, shaking his head. "I guess you could put it that way Marshal. I feel as though I've swallowed something rotten."

"I'm headed on into town right now," Jenks said. "I'll see if I can convince the town marshal to lock your brother up before he tries anything else."

The three men waved and called good-bye to Anne Marie and Bryce. Dan could hardly see as he whipped up the horses. His eyes burned with unshed tears as he sped out of the driveway and back to the public road.

Chapter Eleven

The afternoon was almost gone when Dan and Henry returned to the boardinghouse. They agreed to meet Jenks at the town marshal's office early the next day. All three men stood outside the office door waiting when a deputy arrived to open up the next morning.

"Good morning, fellas, you sure are bright and early. Come on inside. How can I help you?"

Marshal Jenks led the group inside and pulled back his coat to show his badge. "We've got us a serious problem, Deputy," he said, "and we need your help. We've got proof of a crime and we know exactly where the culprit is. We want you or someone from your office to go with us to apprehend him."

"This person is here in St. Louis?"

"Yes. He's resides in the townhouse of a Mr. Julian Devereaux."

"Now you just wait a minute here, Marshal. You're saying Mr. Devereaux is harboring a criminal?"

"No, that ain't what I'm saying at all, sonny. I'm saying Mr. Devereaux's brother, Andre Devereaux, is a criminal, and I've been told that he's staying in his brother's townhouse."

"You people are simply out of your mind if you think I'm going to arrest Julian Devereaux's brother."

"Remember I said I had proof?" Jenks asked, almost shouting.

The office door opened and an older man wearing a town marshal badge walked in. When he caught sight of Jenks' face he let out a wild yell and rushed across the room to grab his hand. "Where in the devil have you been so long, you old sidewinder?"

"Here and there, old friend. Same as always, here and there."

"I'm downright glad to see you're still alive, Jenks. It must be five years or more since I ran into you up in Springfield."

"It's all of that and maybe some more. We're here because we need your help, Randy."

"You've got it, whatever you need. Tell me what's going on."

The deputy stood up from behind the desk to push past Jenks and stand close to the marshal. "Marshal Tucker, these men are trying to charge one of the Devereaux brothers with some sort of crime."

"What's he talking about, Jenks?"

Jenks looked at the deputy with disgust before he turned to his friend. "Here's the story, Randy, and it's a lowdown one. Devereaux's brother Andre paid a fella to kidnap his niece Anne Marie and kill her. When the fella didn't kill the girl and Devereaux found out, he tracked the man down and killed him. Then he tried to kidnap the girl again, and threatened to kill her. We've got proof of everything I say and we know where the man is. We want you to go with us to pick him up and hold him for trial."

"My lord, Jenks. That's one of the finest old families in St. Louis. You better be absolutely sure."

"I'm sure, Randy—plumb sure. Here, read these letters." Jenks held out the roll of papers. "They're in date order and they tell the whole story, up to the time I came into the picture. When you finish reading 'em I'll tell you the rest of it."

Marshal Tucker read the letters slowly. His expression grew more and more horrified as he turned the pages. "This is almost beyond belief. I wouldn't hardly believe anybody could be this lowdown if I read it in a book."

"It's beyond understanding for me, too. Here, Randy, I forgot my manners, let me introduce these boys I've got with me. This is Henry and Dan Smithson—boys, meet Randy Tucker, an old friend. Randy, these boys were part of the rest of the story and I'd like Dan here to tell you what all happened."

Dan started with the night he found the two children hiding in that thicket. He explained the details of everything that happened, up to and including the night Devereaux and his men attacked the ranch house and Devereaux tried to steal Anne Marie.

When Dan finished telling his story Randy Weston turned to his deputy. "Go get our horses ready. It's sure hard to believe this story, but I can't refute this evidence either. Let's get mounted and go arrest Devereaux. He sounds like the kind of crook that'll be long gone if we ain't careful."

When Marshal Tucker rang the bell at the Devereaux townhouse the housekeeper opened the door. She stared at the men fearfully.

"We want to see Andre Devereaux please, ma'am," Marshal Tucker said, removing his hat.

"I'm sorry, sir. Mr. Andre is not here."

"He's not here? When did he leave?"

"He left sometime last night, I can't tell you what time, because I don't know. Mr. Andre came here to recover from a gunshot wound he got while he was fighting Indians somewhere out in Kansas. He'd been getting better, but he still needed to rest. I hadn't the slightest idea he was planning to leave here. He didn't say a word to me—in fact, I didn't even know he'd left the house until I went into his room with his breakfast this morning. I could hardly believe my eyes when I found his room empty."

"Did he leave a note?"

"No, sir. He just left."

"Do you have any idea why he would suddenly leave like that?"

"Not really, sir. All I know is a tall black man came to the door and asked to see him late yesterday evening. He didn't stay in there with Mr. Devereaux but about three minutes. I did notice that Mr. Devereaux seemed a little upset when the man left, but he certainly didn't say anything to me about leaving. He went on to bed just like he normally does."

Tucker thanked the woman. As soon as she shut the door

he turned to the Jenks and his deputy and said, "Let's go men, we've got work to do."

Jenks stopped at the end of the walk and looked back at the beautiful three-story house, a concerned expression on his face. "What do you plan to do now, Randy?"

"What I would ordinarily do. I'll put out the word to all my men to watch the town. Then I'll telegraph down the line for other lawmen to watch out for Devereaux. I know what he looks like, so a description is no problem."

"I've got a feeling he'll already be out of your town," Jenks said. "I've even got a feeling I know where he'll be heading."

"If you have any idea about where to catch up with him I want to go with you."

"It's all right with me, but you're a town marshal, your authority ends when you leave St. Louis proper. I'm a deputy United States Marshal. My regular territory might be eastern Kansas, but I take my authority with me wherever I need to go."

"But shouldn't you at least let the county sheriff know if you're going to be chasing a man in his county?"

"You go on and tell him if you're so worried about it, Randy. I'm taking the Smithson boys with me and going to arrest Devereaux, if he's where I think he is."

Jenks spun on his heel and went to untie his horse. "Come on, boys. We need to ride out to that Château d'Arc."

Dan pushed his horse up near the marshal's. "Why? What's happened, Jenks? Where's Devereaux?"

"Andre Devereaux left here sometime last night. He may have had someone watching for us, I don't know. According to the housekeeper he had a late visitor yesterday evening and disappeared sometime in the night."

Dan didn't say a word. Settling himself in the saddle he whipped his horse to a canter and turned toward the river road. As soon as he cleared the town he put his horse to a full gallop. Henry and Marshal Jenks rode right behind him.

The men left their lathered horses at the brick gates. Taking their rifles, they trotted along the edge of the driveway, keeping close to the row of cedars to let the shadows hide them. The windows of the big house were dark.

"Look at that, will you," Dan whispered, trying to swallow his fear, "this place should be lit up bright as day." His chest hurt—it felt as though a vise clamped down on his ribs—he couldn't seem to get a full breath.

Where is Anne Marie?

"Take it easy, boy, don't jump to no conclusions," Jenks said, keeping his voice low. "That's a big house, those folks might all be to the back somewhere. We wouldn't see those lights from here. I'll stay around here and watch the front door. You and Henry go around the house and meet at the back. If you need me give a whistle.

"Say, do one of you boys remember that black man's name? The one that was out on the porch with Devereaux."

"I think I heard Anne Marie call him Joshua," Henry said. "Why do you want to know that?"

"I sorta thought that if I run into him it would help if I know his name."

Henry leveled his rifle and started toward the north corner of the house. "You might have something there, Marshal—let's go."

Dan stepped around the rear corner of the house. A lamp glowed in a window on the first floor. He moved away from the back of the house far enough to cross the rear yard outside the bright shaft of light. When he came back close to the house at the far corner, he could hear slight rustling movements in the boxwoods.

"Henry—is that you?"

"Yes. Did you find anything?"

"There's a light in that window at the back of the house. I'm going up on that porch over there to try the back door."

"I'll be right behind you."

Dan stepped up on the porch. A board creaked under his feet. He stood still and listened. No one moved inside. He stepped closer to the door. He could hear voices. He couldn't make out any words, only soft murmurs. It sounded like two men talking.

He turned the doorknob and pushed gently against the door. It gave and opened a narrow crack, enough for him to see through. It was too dark for him to see anything at first. He opened the door farther and stuck his head inside the hall. A light gleamed under a closed door on his right.

Henry put his hand on Dan's shoulder. He turned to whisper, "Keep on coming, Hank. I've got to get close enough to figure out who that is doing the talking."

Suddenly Dan heard Anne Marie's voice. She sobbed between words. She sounded almost hysterical. He walked faster. Keeping close to the wall, he carried his pistol in his hand, ready to fire.

Someone opened the door to the lit room and stepped out into the hall. He turned to gently close the door behind him. It was the black man they called Joshua. He carried a tray with the remains of a meal. When he turned away from the door, he saw Dan and Henry and stopped to stare.

He didn't say a word. Shaking his head, he walked toward them. Just before he reached Dan he crossed the hall to open a door that led to the kitchen. He sat the tray he carried on the table, lit a lamp and turned to motion to Dan and Henry to follow him inside. As soon as they came in he closed the door.

"Gentlemen, you are mad to try this, but you may be in time to save the lives of Mr. Devereaux and his daughter. Mr. Andre is in the study with them. He sent me to get him some brandy. I must hurry back. He's holding a pistol on Mr. Julian.

"Miss Anne Marie is sitting on the floor beside her father's chair. He has her trussed up like a pig. He used the drapery cords. Mr. Andre is threatening to shoot her and Mr. Julian. He's talking wild, raving about what he would to do to them."

"Joshua, can you pretend to trip and drop your tray and that drink in Andre Devereaux's lap?" Dan asked.

"Do you think he'll shoot me?"

"He might. I'll give you that, but think about this—if he does shoot your employer and his daughter in front of you do you think he'll let you live?"

Joshua stared at Dan for a moment. "I'll do it." He sounded scared but determined. "I'll shout when I trip and you men rush in and capture him. All right?"

"That'll be perfect," Dan said, patting Joshua on his shoulder. "Go ahead on in there now—we'll be right behind you."

Dan and Henry waited outside the study door, guns ready. Joshua walked past them, looking straight ahead. He held the tray with a footed crystal glass about a quarter full of brandy. He left the door slightly open.

Dan heard Joshua's firm footsteps as he walked toward the middle of the room. There was a loud crash and Joshua and Andre Devereaux both yelled. Devereaux screamed in anger and Joshua began to apologize over and over.

Dan stepped into the study with Henry on his heels. He rushed across the open space to grapple with Devereaux. Grasping the man's wrist and twisting with both hands, he strained to force him to drop his gun. Devereaux fell back in his chair and the sudden force of his weight pulled his wrist out of Dan's hands.

He struck out at Dan with the barrel of the pistol but missed his face and struck him heavily on his shoulder. The momentum of the vicious swing threw Devereaux out of the chair to the floor. He rolled to Dan's left and scrambled up almost instantly to dart toward the open window at the back of the room.

"Stop him," Dan yelled and lunged across the open space with his arms outstretched but missed the man. Devereaux leaped through the open window. The next instant Dan heard a yell and two shots outside.

"Look out, Marshal, he's right behind you." Randy Tucker's voice sounded strained, as though he called from a long distance.

Anne Marie ran into Dan's arms as he turned to see if she was all right. "Henry untied me. Oh, Dan—I knew you'd come—I told Poppa you'd come."

Dan folded his arms around her and held her close. Trembling with relief, he dropped his cheek to rest on her smooth hair. He closed his eyes for a moment, then sighed and lifted his head. He met the angry stare of Julian Devereaux. His message was clear. Anne Marie's father was not pleased to see his daughter in Dan's arms.

Dan stepped back to reach up and slide Anne Marie's arms from his neck, returning Devereaux's stare the whole time.

"I see that I owe you another debt, young man," Devereaux said. "You and your brother seem to have formed a habit of saving my daughter from harm. I offered you a reward earlier. I offer it again."

Henry's voice almost shook with his irritation at Devereaux's insult to his brother. "We didn't do this for money." Henry moved to stand near Dan as he continued, "We told you that earlier, sir." He turned to Dan, "It's time for us to leave."

Anne Marie rushed to face her father. "Stop them, Poppa—please. Stop being so stuck-up. These men are my good friends. I love Dan Smithson and I intend to marry him as soon as I'm eighteen."

Dan jerked around to stare at her in astonishment, his face white.

"You will go to your room, young lady," Devereaux shouted angrily and pounded on the arm of his wheelchair. "All of this noise and madness has made you hysterical. Joshua, you will escort Miss Anne Marie to her room this instant."

"There's no need for you to scream at me, Poppa. You simply don't want to accept how much I've grown up and changed since I've been away. I am not going to my room— you must understand me. I'm going to stay here and tell my friends good-bye and thank them properly for saving me from Uncle Andre."

Turning to face Dan and Henry, Anne Marie held her head high and ignored her father. "I'll walk out with you." She took Dan's arm and headed for the door. "We'll go out through the front of the house."

The sound of a shot reverberated in the room. All three whirled around to look back at Devereaux. He slumped against the left arm of his wheelchair, then slid limply from the seat of the chair to sprawl on the floor. Almost immediately another shot sounded. A large splinter flew up from the door beside Anne Marie's head.

Dan grabbed her arms at almost the same instant and shoved her through the door and out into the hallway where she couldn't be seen from the window. "Stay here where you're safe. There's no need to try to get to your father. You can't help him. That shot caught him on the side of his head. I'm going out the front door and around to the back of the house. I've got to find out what's going on.

"Henry, stay here with Anne Marie, please. I'm going around to find out how Devereaux got away from Marshal Jenks."

Easing open the front door, Dan let himself out, ignoring Henry's protests. Holding his pistol high, he raced around the house. He slowed to a walk when he reached the back corner and leaned against the bricks to peer around the corner at the lit area near the window the shot came through.

He could see the outline of a body on the ground close to the window. No one else was in sight. He called out, "Marshal, where are you?"

Randy Tucker answered him. His voice came from the dimness near the carriage house at the back of the garden.

"Jenks is bad hurt, Dan. He's lying on the ground right there behind the house, underneath that window."

"What happened, for God's sake? Where the devil is Andre Devereaux? I thought you had him."

Walking quickly, Randy came closer to Dan so he could talk normally. "He's gone, Smithson—got clean away. Jenks almost got him, but Devereaux shot him. The marshal's got at least one bullet in his chest, I think another one hit his shoulder.

"Jenks put a slug in Devereaux after he was down, but it didn't stop him. I tried to catch the skunk, but he ran into the woods near the river. I'll have to go to town and get a doctor for the marshal and round up some men and dogs to help me track Devereaux."

Dan rushed over to kneel beside Marshal Jenks. Placing his right hand on his shoulder, he asked, "How are you, Marshal?"

Jenks groaned and tried to lift his head. "Where's Randy, Dan?"

"He's right here with me, Marshal. Don't try to talk."

"I've got something to say that needs a witness."

Horrified, Dan realized his hand was wet with the marshal's blood. He struck a match. Jenk's face was gray, and his entire chest and shoulder dripped red. Dan could hear air whistling from the wound in his chest.

"You take my guns, Dan, all of 'em. I want you to have them." The whistling was louder, and Jenks' voice sounded strained. "Finish writing my report and send it in to Springfield for me, okay?"

"Of course I will. Stop worrying about things like that,

Marshal. Randy's going to St. Louis to get a doctor for you. He'll patch you up and you'll be able to take care of things yourself in a few days."

"No—no I won't, son. I'm almost out of breath." Jenks' voice was a whisper. Dan had to lean close to his face to hear. "Take the guns, boy, and the things in my saddlebags. Promise me you will."

"I promise, Jenks." Hot tears slid down Dan's face. He wiped his wet hand on the grass. Jenks gasped and shuddered and his head fell to the side, pulling away from Dan's hand. Striking another match, Dan saw that Jenks' eyes were fixed. He seemed to be staring straight at him.

"He's gone, Randy."

"God, I'm sorry."

"He was a good friend," Dan said. "I'd gotten to feel kinda close to him."

"I'll wrap him up in a blanket and get him up on his horse so we can take him in to the undertaker."

"Where would he be buried?"

"There's a big graveyard west of town."

"Andre Devereaux killed his brother, blew the side of his head off."

"I heard the shots and came running around the corner of the house. Devereaux stood right there at the window. Jenks shot him just as he turned around to run away. He half-turned back as he ran and shot at the marshal twice.

"I was a good distance away. I shot, but missed the devil. I kept on chasing him until he disappeared into the brush and trees down near the edge of the river. I'll go on into town and get the sheriff and some more men. The sheriff's got a pack of dogs. We'll find him."

The back door of the house opened and Anne Marie came running out holding a lantern high, Joshua and Henry were right behind her. Rushing down the steps, she came over to stand beside Dan.

She placed one hand on Dan's arm. "I heard you and Marshal Tucker talking, Dan. I'm so sorry about Marshal Jenks."

She turned to Randy. "Marshal Tucker, don't even think of moving him into town. Marshal Jenks was our dear friend and there's plenty of room in the Château burial ground for him. Please find Father Michael and bring him back here with you. He'll bring the undertaker and he can read the service for both men. On second thought, you'd better find old Neil Bigelow and bring him out here as well. He's—I mean he was—my father's lawyer."

Turning to Joshua she said, "You and your sons go prepare a grave for my father. You know where he wanted his resting place. Please prepare Marshal Jenks' grave close to the fence on the other side of the plot, near that old stone obelisk."

As sad as he felt, Dan still had to smile at the high-handed way Anne Marie spoke and acted. He pictured the smart-mouthed young boy he thought he'd found hiding in that thicket. She had tried to make him believe she was an ignorant kid from the backcountry so he'd leave her alone. Now she was acting and sounding like a proud St. Louis lady.

"Come in the house, Dan. I'll have Joshua's wife prepare rooms for you and Henry. I want you to stay here with me. If you still have some things in town, make arrangements for Marshal Tucker to bring them back out here for you. I won't feel safe for a moment unless you're here with me."

"I guess we'd better stay here until Randy captures your

uncle," Dan said, "but will anything be said about us being here with your father dead?"

"The servants and your brother are chaperone enough for me. Not that I care a whit what any nosy busybody might say about me." Anne Marie tossed her head and turned to lead the way back into the house. Someone had closed the door to the room that held Julian Devereaux's body.

Chapter Twelve

It was almost noon the next day when Henry shook Dan's shoulder and said, "There's a couple of buggies coming up the lane—let's get on downstairs. I'd just as soon whoever that is not know I slept most of the day away."

"You're right there. It makes us look sort of sorry like, even if we were up most of the night. Whew, I slept like I'd been hit over the head."

"Well, hurry up and get ready."

Dan and Henry were both dressed and sitting at the dining room table when they heard the sound of the doorknocker. Joshua poured each of them a cup of coffee and placed a platter of rolls within their reach.

"There's plenty of coffee and rolls here, gentlemen. Miss Anne Marie will be down soon and I'll serve your dinner. I expect the two men at the door will be glad of something to sustain them. I've never known either one of those gentlemen to turn down a meal in this house."

A younger black man stepped in the dining room door and announced, "Mr. Bigelow and Father Michael McClain."

Dan and Henry stood up at their places to greet the two men. Bigelow eyed them with a frown and Father McClain nodded. The lawyer and priest immediately took seats on the opposite side of the table from the brothers.

Bigelow spoke first. "I am going to venture a guess that you're the Smithson brothers, the men who rescued Miss Devereaux and returned her to her home. Am I correct?"

Henry nodded in return. "You're correct, sir. I'm Henry Smithson and this is my brother Daniel. We found Anne Marie and brought her back home."

"Marshal Tucker told us that Mr. Julian Devereaux was murdered by his brother Andre. I notified the undertaker. He'll be along early this afternoon. The marshal will back here soon as well. He started out ahead of us with a bunch of men and a pack of hounds. We saw them turn off toward the river about a mile before we reached the gate of the château."

"I certainly hope he finds Devereaux. That man has caused Anne Marie enough trouble," Dan said, grimly.

"Yes—yes. You're right about that, Mr. Smithson. This is an awful business. I wonder if you could tell me when you plan to leave here?"

"I won't be leaving here until Andre Devereaux is dead or captured. I believe the man is completely mad. He's so set on inheriting this place he's proven that he'll stop at nothing to get it. I'm not about to leave here until I know Anne Marie is safe." Dan's voice held a note of steel and his determination was obvious in his stern expression.

"Andre Devereaux is a fool. I've always believed he was a

little bit off. When Julian married again and had that child. . . . I think you're probably correct. Knowing he was no longer his brother's heir drove him completely mad. I tried to tell him that he would be taken care of in his brother's will, but he would never believe me.

"It was impossible for me to tell him exactly what Julian planned, it wouldn't have been ethical. Andre got so upset when Miss Anne Marie was born, I felt then that I should try to reassure him, but he flatly refused to believe what I could tell him and I couldn't explain fully." Bigelow sounded nervous and his words came out in a rush.

All four men rose to their feet and turned to face the door as a soft step and a rustle of skirts preceded Anne Marie in the door. She smiled and walked close to Bigelow and Father McClain to curtsey. "I'm so glad you could come, gentlemen. Please be seated, everyone. I've ordered dinner. It won't be but a few more minutes."

She walked around the table, holding out her hand to Dan. He still stood beside his chair. "Good morning, my dear," she said, smiling up at him, "I hope you slept well."

Dan glanced at the blank faces of the two men across the table as he took Anne Marie's hand and smiled down at her. "We both did. I'm embarrassed to say how long I slept. Henry had to shake me awake when he saw your visitors coming down the lane."

Anne Marie laughed up at him. Her eyes clung to his. Dan wanted to grab her in his arms and hold her. She finally pulled her hand out of his and turned to settle into a chair at the end of the table.

Still smiling, she turned to Bigelow. "I've arranged to have my father's funeral this afternoon. I am counting on the undertaker getting here between one and two o'clock to make the necessary preparations. My father's funeral will be followed by the funeral of a dear friend who died defending me from Uncle Andre. I hope you and Father Michael are prepared to stay overnight. It will probably be quite late when everything is over."

Father McClain answered, "Of course we'll stay, my dear. You shouldn't be alone in your grief. I asked several members of my congregation to let your father's friends know about this tragedy. I am sure some of them will start arriving soon, they'll want to pay their respects to your father and help to console you."

"How very kind of you, Father," Anne Marie said. "I'll have Joshua prepare rooms for both of you and make sure to have the cook prepare your favorite foods for supper."

"You look so much like your mother, child."

"I'm no longer a child, Father. You forget that I'm seventeen years old."

Bigelow leaned forward to smile at Anne Marie. "You do look amazingly like your mother, Anne Marie. She would be very proud of you.

"You must remember, however, you're still a child in the eyes of the law, and I'm the fortunate person your father appointed to be your guardian. I'll be responsible for your welfare until your marriage."

"I thought that might be the case, Mr. Bigelow. That's why I asked Marshal Tucker to contact you this morning. You should know that Mr. Dan Smithson is my affianced husband. We plan to marry immediately and return to Kansas."

Dan strangled on a swallow of coffee and covered his

cough with his napkin. When he cleared his throat so he could speak and raised his head everyone at the table was staring at him. Henry looked at him with his mouth open. Bigelow and the reverend father simply looked indignant. Anne Marie's expression was serious, but her eyes held a dancing light.

"Isn't that right, Dan?" she asked as she turned to smile at Dan.

Dan couldn't speak. He felt a crazy impulse to laugh out loud. Swallowing hard, he stared at her and nodded his agreement.

Joshua walked into the room holding a loaded tray and began to serve the meal. Feeling he'd been given a reprieve, Dan concentrated on his plate. He heard Anne Marie's voice, and the lawyer and the priest talking during the meal, but their voices were no more than muddled sounds. None of what they said made any sense.

When Joshua removed the plates and served small cups of black coffee, the shock had begun to wear off. Dan glanced over at Henry. When he met his brother's laughing eyes Dan had to immediately hold his napkin over his mouth again, this time to hide his own grin.

Turning to Anne Marie, Dan said, "I hear horses. It's not a wagon, so it must be Marshal Tucker and the posse. Please excuse us."

"Of course. I hope you'll hurry back and tell me what's happened. If it is the posse please send the men around to the back porch. Joshua fried some chicken and made bread and coffee for them. They're bound to be hungry."

Pushing their chairs back, Dan and Henry left the table.

They hurried down the hall toward the back door, grabbing their hats from the hall tree as they passed. When Dan opened the door Randy Tucker stepped up on the back porch.

Tucker looked exhausted. He removed his hat and shook his head when he met Dan's eyes. Pulling a red handkerchief out of his coat pocket, he wiped his forehead before he spoke. "I hate to tell you boys this, but we missed Devereaux some kinda way.

"I turned the dogs loose as soon as we got to the woods and they went straight to the river. He had a canoe or boat tied up under some trees. We found where he pulled it up on the bank. I reckon that's how he got here in the first place.

"Two of my men are out on the river in a skiff we found tied up at the château dock right now, looking for him. I'm afraid he could be miles away by now. To tell the truth," Tucker said, shaking his head in disgust, "he coulda holed up somewhere nearby—it's hard to tell what a man like that might do. He coulda hid that boat in some creek right here on château property and be watching us right this minute."

"Well, that's a heck of a note. Don't fuss yourself about it, Randy," Dan said, "we know you did all you could. What do you think we should do now?"

"Stay on your guard, Smithson, that's all I can tell you. I've got to release the posse and git on back to town, but I wouldn't bet on that crazy man leaving you alone. You might want to see if you can hire some of the men riding in the posse to help you guard the house."

"You can't stay a little longer? At least 'til tomorrow?"

"I can't do any more here, Dan. I've got work waiting for me in town. I'll be notifying the U.S. Marshal's Office about Jenks' death. I'll also tell them about Devereaux getting away and ask for some help, but I know from experience that it'll take several days at least for anybody to get here. I'll send some more men out in a boat when I get back to town to see if they can spot Devereaux. They'll find him if he's on the river. You're going to have to keep a guard on this house day and night until Devereaux is captured. I can't see no other way."

"Do you really think he'd try to get in the house again?" Dan asked, pushing his hat back.

"I wouldn't put a doggone thing past that man, and you shouldn't either. He's not backed off from a thing yet as far as I've seen. I can't help but figure that a man that'll shoot his own brother to get his hands on a piece of land and a house'll do most anything."

"I guess I better go back in and tell Anne Marie the news. I don't look forward to it, I'll tell you that."

"I'll stay outside with Marshal Tucker while you go talk to her, Dan," Henry said. "Maybe I can hire two or three of these men to stay here and help us for a few days."

"Thanks, Henry. Don't forget to tell them about the fried chicken. I'll see you later—take care, Randy."

Dan stepped back inside the house and closed the door. He could hear loud voices in the dining room. He hurried along the hall and stepped into the room. Bigelow and Father Mc-Clain were standing beside Anne Marie's chair leaning over her. Both of them were talking at once.

"Would you gentlemen care to tell me what the problem is here?" Dan's voice rang out loud and rough. He felt a fierce surge of anger that seemed to carry him to the other side of Anne Marie's chair in one step. He reached down and took one of her hands, then turned to glower at the two men.

Bigelow showed all the symptoms of panic. His face flushed and his voice became loud and high-pitched. He straightened up to his full height to shake his finger at Dan. Almost babbling, he said, "I am this child's guardian, sir. She will not be marrying you tomorrow. I forbid it—I absolutely forbid it—and you should know that I control her property by her father's will."

"Mr. Bigelow, if Anne Marie wants to marry me you'll have no say about it. I'm a rancher and I live a simple life, but I can provide her with everything she needs. She doesn't have to have her father's property or money. I don't care about that, but you better understand this, if you raise your voice to her again I'll give you the beating of your life."

Turning to the priest Dan continued, "I mean that for you, too, Father McClain. I'm not a bit surprised by a lawyer acting this way, but I'm plain shocked and disappointed to see you bullying this girl."

Anne Marie stood up and stuck both hands up in front of her, with her palms out. "All of you, please—please hush. Stop this. You're making me feel sick with your wrangling."

Stepping close to Dan, she said, "It's all right Dan, really it is. Mr. Bigelow and Father Michael are just concerned about me. They didn't frighten me and they can't make me do anything I don't want to do. That's the very reason they raised their voices."

Dan turned to smile down at Anne Marie. Ignoring the two men, he grasped her shoulders with both hands. "Anne Marie, I came in here to tell you that your Uncle Andre got away from the posse. Marshal Tucker thinks it's possible that he might try to get in the house again. Henry's out there now trying to hire some of the men that were riding in the posse to help us guard the house until we can catch him."

"Oh, my Lord, I so hoped it was all over." She dropped her head and leaned against Dan. "I'll swear, I don't know how much longer I can stand this."

"It's all right, Anne Marie, I promise. We'll take care of you. I'm just grateful we're still here in the house where we can keep you safe. If Henry can hire one or two more men to help us we'll be able to cover the house. I don't reckon he'd be able to get by us."

"Uncle Andre has to be mad."

"I couldn't argue with that."

"I've got to go take care of some things," Anne Marie said. "The undertaker came in while you were outside. He's preparing Father and Marshal Jenks now. I set the funeral for three o'clock. We'll have Father's first and then Marshal Jenks'. I want to attend their burials."

"All right. I noticed some men riding up the lane as I came in. Why don't you let Bigelow and McClain here handle them so you can go rest some until everything is ready?"

"That's an excellent idea, thank you."

Anne Marie turned to address the lawyer. "Mr. Bigelow— will you greet the guests who will be at the door soon? I'm sure they've come to pay their respects to my father. Please invite them into the parlor to the left of the front hall and pull the bell for Joshua. He'll bring them something to drink."

"Er, ahh—of course, Miss Devereaux, I'd be delighted." Bigelow kept his head down as he answered, averting his eyes from both Dan and Anne Marie. His reaction to Dan's harshness still showed in his red face and the tone of his voice. He nodded to Father McClain and proceeded him out of the room.

"Are you sure you should be so determined with that lawyer? You're probably entitled to this house and all the things that go with it. You know I can't give you anything like this."

"I know what's in my father's will, Dan. Mr. Bigelow can't do a thing except what I tell him to do after I marry, and he has nothing to do with choosing my husband. You do want to marry me, don't you?"

"You know how I feel. Of course I want to marry you— today, tomorrow—as soon as you're willing."

Anne Marie smiled up at him. "I want to get married to-morrow and go back to the Triangle Eight with you."

"That's fine with me, but what about this house and every-thing? Won't there be business you need to take care of?"

"I'll get Bigelow to take care of everything. It's ironic, Dan. Uncle Andre threw his life away to get Château d'Arc, when the whole time, father's will provided that he would control this property for his lifetime, then it would come to me.

"It's a shame really, if he'd only been willing to wait a short time. When I went through Father's papers this morn-ing I found several letters from doctors. His illness was much worse than most people knew. My father only had a few months to live."

"I guess it is a shame about your uncle, but some people ask for their own trouble."

"Oh, there's an interesting thing in Father's will. He left a property called Beverly to Mildred Gillis and also the mill property adjacent to it. He referred to Mildred as his cousin and said she was his wife Victoria's best friend. My mother's name was Victoria. I think that might go a long way to explaining why Mildred Gillis protected me from her husband."

"That's the property described in those deeds Gillis kept in that basket, isn't it?"

"Yes, I gave them to Mr. Bigelow. I can't explain why Gillis had them though, that just doesn't make any sense."

"Well, I certainly don't know, but I would guess he stole them out of your father's office."

"I'm truly pleased that Bryce will be well provided for, aren't you?"

"Of course I am. Where'd that boy get to anyway?"

"He's up in my old nursery playing with my toys. A young girl from the next plantation is looking after him. I sent Joshua's son Adam over to there to borrow several people to work in the house when I got up this morning. I knew there'd be a lot of people to feed after the funeral. Joshua and his family couldn't begin to handle everything alone."

"Why don't you go on and rest until you have to change for the funeral. I'll go outside and see if Henry hired some of those men to help us guard the house."

"You'll walk with me to the graveyard?"

"Of course I will," Dan said.

Dozens of mourners attended Julian Devereaux's funeral. They were mostly men, but a few women gathered together at the rear of the group. Dan stood beside Anne Marie but kept his eyes moving, watching the crowd on the other side of the grave. He knew Henry did the same thing beside him. They would both be nervous until Devereaux was caught.

Most of the mourners drifted back to the house after Devereaux's burial, but about two dozen were curious enough to follow Anne Marie and the Smithson brothers to the grave prepared for Marshal Jenks. When Father McClain finished giving the service for the marshal, Henry stepped up to the head of the grave.

Clearing his throat, he read from a small slip of paper. "Lord, we got to know Marshal Jenks because we had trouble and he came to help us. He was our friend and died while protecting one of us. He'll be remembered. Amen."

Anne Marie squeezed Dan's arm and smiled at Henry. "That was truly beautiful, Henry. Thank you."

Dan couldn't speak. His heart was too full. He moved closer to the grave and dropped a handful of dirt on the coffin, then turned and walked away, still holding Anne Marie's hand.

"I'll have to go into the parlor and talk to some of my father's friends. I hate it, but it's got to be done. That'll probably take me an hour, then we'll go to the library and let Mr. Bigelow read the will, even though I've already read it. He claims it's a rule, to have a special reading, and he's set on doing things the right way."

"What do you reckon will happen to this property," Dan asked, "since it's supposed to go to your uncle until he dies?"

"Lord knows. I seem to remember reading somewhere that a murderer can't profit from his victim's will."

"I think you're probably right about that. I reckon Bigelow'll know what to do."

"Why don't you wait outside while I do this, Dan? You don't know any of these people, and standing in a receiving line is about as boring as anything can get."

"You're sure you'll be all right in there alone?"

"I'll be fine. You go ahead and talk with Henry. I'm sure you want to make plans for guarding the house tonight."

"You go ahead then. I'll wait here for Henry. Oh, here he comes now."

"I hired three men," Henry said as he reached Dan's side, "all three of them have got a rifle and a handgun. I promised them five dollars a day and a fifty-dollar bonus to the man that gets Devereaux. They're guarding the doors right now. I was kinda afraid that Devereaux would try to get inside the house when we were all at the funerals."

"That's good thinking—I'm relieved. I hope you're feeling rested enough to sit up all night. I thought I'd just take me one of those feather ticks to wrap up in and lean against Anne Marie's door all night tonight myself. I'd like for you to find a place to keep a watch downstairs, if you will."

"I've already planned that out. If you sit at Anne Marie's door and I stay downstairs and sort of patrol around to check on all the windows, we should have it covered. Those windows worry me, they're built so low a tall man could almost step up over the sill and walk right in the house."

"We can check every one and make sure they're locked," Dan said. "If they're all locked, Devereaux would have to make some noise to get through one of them."

"Yeah. I'll check them."

Dan rubbed his hand over his face. "Henry, I'm getting married tomorrow."

"You're what?"

"Me and Anne Marie are getting married tomorrow. She's coming back to Kansas with us."

"Well, just where do you expect to live when you get there? You know I'm marrying Bella as soon as we get back home. She and Inez are making her dress right now. I'd planned on you moving to the old foreman's cabin and letting us take over the house."

"You do exactly what you want, Henry Smithson, that's what you always do anyway. Me and Anne Marie can find our own accommodations."

"Now don't be like that, Dan. You know how much I need you on the ranch. You can't up and leave on me."

"I can leave you if I want to, Henry. It might be helpful for you to remember that fact. I don't want to leave, though. Believe it or not, I care as much about that place as you do. The only thing that would make me think of leaving the Triangle Eight would be for you to keep on trying to treat me like I'm about ten years old.

"Anne Marie and me can live in the old foreman's cabin until we can build us our own place. I've always wanted to build me a house in that spot I like over near the eastern fence. You know where I mean, where those three springs are, in that grove of sycamore trees."

"As long as you don't leave. I'll learn to treat you like a partner, I swear I will."

"That'll be great, Hank. You never did answer my question—will you stand up with me tomorrow?"

"You know I will. Say, have you thought that . . . you and that girl both are getting married awful young?"

"Leave it alone, brother. I don't want to hear it. Let's go on in the house."

The hall clock struck midnight as Dan wrapped the tick around his shoulders and sat down on the floor, resting his back against the door of Anne Marie's bedroom. Some of the mourners had stayed for the reading of the will, enjoying Julian Devereaux's whiskey. After the reading was over, Father McClain and Lawyer Bigelow closeted themselves with Anne Marie to argue over what to do with her property. When she insisted that Dan sit beside her during the interview the two men were careful to keep their voices calm and soft.

The three men Henry hired from the posse guarded the front, back and side doors of the house. Dan could hear Henry's step occasionally as he walked from one side of the house to the other, checking windows. The only other sounds he heard were the intermittent screech of an owl and the faraway yapping of a fox.

Hours passed. Almost asleep, Dan heard something— something that yanked him awake and made him instantly alert. He grasped his pistol and stood up to listen, dropping the feather tick from his shoulders. He heard the sound again. A board creaked. Again, the creaks seemed to be moving—they had to be someone's footsteps on the second floor. The creaking noises were close by, but at first Dan couldn't place their direction. Cold with fear, he turned to place his ear against one of the panels of Anne Marie's door.

Maybe it's the sound of the house settling. Maybe I'm just nervous. No—no, there it goes again.

Someone was creeping along, placing each foot carefully to make as little noise as possible. Slowly turning the knob, Dan eased Anne Marie's door open enough to slip through, thankful there were no lamps burning to give away his position. He closed the door silently and leaned back against it to steady himself, breathing as quietly as possible.

After a moment he could hear Anne Marie's soft, regular breathing. She still slept. A thin shaft of moonlight painted a streak of brightness across her face. Dan watched with horror as a shadow moved into the dim light to the left of the window. Someone else was in the room.

Heart pounding, Dan raised his pistol and silently moved farther into the room.

The shadow almost reached the middle of the room. The strip of moonlight outlined a man's raised arm and hand. He held a knife high.

Out of the corner of his eye Dan noticed a blur of movement on the bed. Anne Marie had sensed a presence in the room. She jerked awake to sit straight up in the bed, screaming Dan's name.

At the sound of her voice Devereaux leaped toward the bed. He snatched at Anne Marie's arm with his free hand. She screamed and twisted away from him, throwing her body off the far side of the bed and onto the floor.

"Stop where you are, Devereaux," Dan yelled as loud as he could, hoping Henry would hear him and come to help. He felt a searing explosion of anger and fear in his chest. It seemed to propel him across the room. Afraid to use his gun so close to Anne Marie, he dropped it to the floor with his left hand and grabbed for Devereaux with his right.

He caught the wrist of Devereaux's arm in his right hand

and closed his left on the cloth of his vest and shirt. Straining, he pulled him close. Devereaux twisted suddenly and pulled the hand that held the knife out of Dan's grip. He reached for it again and felt the sting of the blade against his forearm. Trying again he caught Devereaux's wrist and twisted it cruelly until the knife clattered to the floor.

Swinging his free hand, Devereaux struck the left side of Dan's face with his closed fist. The shock of the blow almost forced Dan to loosen his grip. Twisting to pull his wrist loose Devereaux fell backward, pulling Dan with him. When they hit the floor Dan shifted the grip of his left hand from Devereaux's clothing to his throat and threw his whole weight behind his hand, pressing down with all his strength. When he felt Devereaux's arm grow limp, he released his wrist and moved his right hand to his throat to press harder.

Light suddenly filled the room. Excited voices began to penetrate the haze of fury and hate that filled Dan. Strong arms pulled at his hands and arms, struggling to release the death grip he held on Devereaux's throat.

"Stop it Dan—stop. It's all right—you can stop now. I've got the knife. Let him go—for God's sake, Dan, let him go. Stop this right now," Henry yelled, his mouth close to Dan's ear.

Removing his hands from Devereaux's throat Dan moved back to a kneeling position and stared down at the man. After a moment, he whispered, "Is he dead?"

Henry moved past Dan and knelt to place two fingers against Devereaux's bruised throat. "Yes. He's dead."

"Good. Get these men to haul his carcass out of here and ask Joshua to fix up another room for Anne Marie."

Trembling in reaction to the harsh grip of fear and anger,

Dan rubbed his face with both hands, covering his eyes. A soft hand touched his cheek. He dropped his hands and looked up. Anne Marie smiled and knelt to slip her arms around his neck. She whispered, "It's over, Dan. It's finally over."